the Cheetah girls

Growl Power

Deborah Gregory

JUMP AT THE SUN

Fashion credits: Photography by Charlie Pizzarello. Models: Mia Lee, Sabrina Millen, Sonya Millen, Imani Parks, and Brandi Stewart. Dresses by Betsey Johnson. Bodysuits by P. Fields and Nicole Miller. Stockings by Sox Trot. Jewelry accessories by Agatha Paris. Hair by Julie McIntosh. Makeup by Lanier Long and Deborah Wallace. Fashion styling by Nole Marin.

Printed in the United States of America
First Edition
1 3 5 7 9 10 8 6 4 2
This book is set in 12-point Palatino.
ISBN: 0-7868-1427-6
Library of Congress Catalog Card Number: 99-067726.
Visit www.cheetahgirls.com

For supa-dupa Davida,
Wait till you meet her
'Cuz you're gonna say,
There's a cheetah
With growl power
Who couldn't be sweeter!

The Cheetah Girls Credo

To earn my spots and rightful place in the world, I solemnly swear to honor and uphold the Cheetah Girls oath:

🐾 Cheetah Girls don't litter, they glitter. I will help my family, friends, and other Cheetah Girls whenever they need my love, support, or a *really* big hug.

🐾 All Cheetah Girls are created equal, but we are not alike. We come in different sizes, shapes, and colors, and hail from different cultures. I will not judge others by the color of their spots, but by their character.

🐾 A true Cheetah Girl doesn't spend more time doing her hair than her homework. Hair extensions may be career extensions, but talent and skills will pay my bills.

🐾 True Cheetah Girls *can* achieve without a weave—or a wiggle, jiggle, or a giggle. I promise to rely (mostly) on my brains, heart, and courage to reach my cheetah-licious potential!

🐾 A brave Cheetah Girl isn't afraid to admit when she's scared. I promise to get on my knees and summon the growl power of the Cheetah Girls who came before me—including my mom, grandmoms, and the Supremes—and ask them to help me be strong.

🐾 All Cheetah Girls make mistakes. I promise to admit when I'm wrong and will work to make it right. I'll also say I'm sorry, even when I don't want to.

🐾 Grown-ups are not always right, but they are bigger, older, and louder. I will treat my teachers, parents, and people of authority with respect—and expect them to do the same!

🐾 True Cheetah Girls don't run with wolves or hang with hyenas. True Cheetahs pick much better friends. I will not try to get other people's approval by acting like a copycat.

🐾 To become the Cheetah Girl that only *I* can be, I promise not to follow anyone else's dreams but my own. No matter how much I quiver, shake, shiver, and quake!

🐾 Cheetah Girls were born for adventure. I promise to learn a language other than my own and travel around the world to meet my fellow Cheetah Girls.

Chapter 1

Angie and I are soooo grateful that school is out for the Thanksgiving holidays! A whole week off this year, too—thanks to construction at our school, LaGuardia Performing Arts League. All we can think about is heading home to Houston, and telling everybody about the Big Apple till they're green with envy!

We, of course, is me, Aquanette Walker, and my twin sister Anginette—but *I'm* usually the one doing the talking, because I can't help *thinking* of the two of us as one person. (It's something you'd understand if people were always confusing *you* for your twin!)

Right now, *we* are fixing up a special dinner

in the kitchen of the big New York City apartment we share with our daddy. We've been living here since June, and already there's been more excitement than we had in all those years back in Houston!

But that doesn't mean we don't want to go back home to visit. Our ma is down there, still living in the old house we love so much. And *her* mama—our grandma, whom we all call "Big Momma," still lives in the house she and Granddaddy Selby lived in for fifty years or more. Granddaddy died seven years ago, but that don't stop Big Momma. *Nothing* stops her!

Granddaddy Walker will be waiting for us, too. Angie and I can't wait to visit the Rest in Peace Funeral Parlor again—that's where he lives! It's granddaddy's business, and he lives up top, two floors above the corpses. I guess that's why our daddy has always been such a serious person—and why Angie and I just loooove horror movies!

The dinner we are fixing is not for our daddy. He wouldn't eat it, so why bother? He only eats the kind of food his new girlfriend makes him—seaweed shakes and stuff like that. Daddy is looking thin and peaked, if you ask me; but he thinks he's never looked better.

I believe he's been bewitched by High Priestess Abala Shaballa Bogo Hexagone. That's his girlfriend's name, believe it or not. She claims to be a real high priestess. I don't know about that, but she sure is strange. I don't like her one bit, and neither does Angie.

Anyway, we're cooking a holiday dinner for the Cheetah Girls right now—that would be Galleria "Bubbles" Garibaldi, Dorinda "Do' Re Mi" Rogers, and Chanel "Chuchie" Simmons. The five of us are a cheetah-licious girl group, and we've got mad skills, too. Being Cheetah Girls is the best thing that ever happened to me and Angie. Not only do we have a crew of our own, but we're close as can be to getting a record contract! Can you believe it?

The first time the Cheetah Girls came over to our house, Princess Abala Shaballa was doing the cooking. She made up this good-luck brew for us out of some nasty roots and herbs. It was supposed to help us win the Apollo Theatre Amateur Hour Contest—which it didn't. We came in second.

Right now, Chanel and Dorinda are sitting at the kitchen table, watching me and Angie do the cooking. Suddenly Chanel stands up and puts her dirty, sneakered foot up on the edge of the sink to stretch it!

Angie and I look at each other like, "Yes, she really is doing that!"

"I've *gotta* stretch my legs, or I'll get rigor mortis, and they'll fall off or something," Chanel giggles. Ever since Chanel and the rest of the Cheetah Girls found out that our grand-daddy owns Rest in Peace Funeral Parlor, they are always trying to take a stab at us with "corpse jokes." Ha, ha, yes, ma'am.

I would say something back, and make her get her feet off my clean sink, but I know Chanel's legs are extra tired. See, she ran in the Junior Gobbler Race in Central Park this morning. She *won*, too! They gave her a big ol' turkey, but she turned around and gave it to Dorinda's foster mother, Mrs. Bosco, so all those foster kids in their house would have turkey for Thanksgiving.

"That was real nice of you to give Dorinda your turkey, Chanel," Angie says, thinking the same thought as me, like always.

"Don't worry, *mamacita*," Chanel says. "At least *someone's* gonna get to eat it—because *I* sure can't eat all of it by myself." Chanel is laughing at the thought of it, making a face like she just ate a whole turkey.

Angie and I are laughing with her, but then I get a look at Dorinda, and I realize she has been sitting like a frog on a log ever since she and Chanel plopped in.

"Are you tired or somethin'?" I ask her. "Did you run in that race, too?"

"I did," she says. "But I'm not tired. I'm just . . ." She heaves a big sigh and looks at Angie and me. "You two are so lucky you're going home for the holidays," she moans.

I guess we do still consider Houston our home, even though we live in the Big Apple. But sometimes it seems like something is missing—I guess it just doesn't feel right without the smell of Ma's Shalimar perfume wafting through the air.

Still, at least *I'm* going home to see *my* ma. Dorinda doesn't even *remember* her real mother. I can see she is depressed. This must be a hard time of year if you're a foster child like Do' Re Mi. She lives with ten other foster kids uptown in Harlem. She likes it there okay, but around the holiday season, I'll bet she misses having a real family—even a split-up one like ours.

"Here, Do' Re Mi, why don't you cut these up?" I say, passing her a knife and chopping board. I figure it's better to put her on onion patrol than have her sitting there looking glum.

Not that we need her help. Angie and I are cookin' this special dinner for our friends without *anybody's* help, thank you.

"I wish *I* was going somewhere for the holidays," Chanel pipes up. "You two get to have all the fun."

Our lives back in Houston may seem glamorous to Chanel, but what she doesn't realize is that Angie and I were sleeping in twin coffins before we became part of the Cheetah Girls—that's how *boring* our lives were. But, like Big Momma says, "the grass always looks greener on the other side."

"Bubbles should be here soon," Chanel says, trying to lick some cream off the spatula.

At least *Galleria* is happy about spending Thanksgiving in New York. That's mostly because her grandmother and favorite aunt—I think her name is Aunt Donie-something (it's hard for me to pronounce)—are flying in from Bologna, Italy.

Imagine that—having family in another country! Now to me, *that* is glamorous. Bubbles is late today because she had to go to the airport with her father, Mr. Garibaldi, to pick the relatives up.

"You gonna eat at Bubbles's house too, right?" I ask Chanel delicately.

"I guess so. *Mamí*'s going to Paris to see her boyfriend—"

"The sheik that makes you shriek?" Dorinda asks, scrunching up her cute little nose.

Chanel's parents are dee-vorced, just like ours, but Ms. Simmons has this strange new boyfriend who lives in Paris, Zurich, *and* Saudi Arabia.

"*Sí, mamacita.* The loony tycoon!" Chanel says, giggling at her own joke. Then she stops smiling and adds in a sad voice, "And Daddy is going to Transylvania with Princess Pamela, to see her family over there."

Princess Pamela is Chanel's father's girlfriend. She has a hair salon and a fortune-telling parlor, and she is quite mysterious—just Angie's and my cup of tea. Chanel is really crazy about her, too. But her father and Pamela didn't invite Chuchie to Romania with them.

They left her home with her *abuela*—her grandma. I know Chanel loves her *abuela*, but I also know she'd rather have gone along to Transylvania.

If you ask me, it's a good thing Galleria's family invited the two of them over. That Abuela Florita of Chanel's is getting too old to cook a big dinner all by herself. And forget about Chanel. I don't think she knows how to make anything except reservations.

"I don't know why y'all are so sad about staying in *New Yawk*," Anginette says to Chanel. "At least you'll have *fun* over at Ms. Dorothea's. Not like at home with your mother."

Chuchie doesn't respond, even though I can see Dorinda is trying to take her side. I know Chanel has problems at home, always fighting with her mom—but nobody told her to run up her mother's credit card behind her back! That isn't exactly the best way to win brownie points!

"At least we've all got some money to spend," I say, trying to cheer Chanel up. You'd think she'd be happy we won a hundred dollars each for coming in second at the Apollo

Theatre in the "Battle of the Divettes" Competition. That's right—we came in second in *that* one, too! It seems like when it comes to the Apollo, the Cheetah Girls always come out second best. Lord, keep me away from that place from now on!

Galleria, Chanel, and even Dorinda were upset that we only came in second. But not me. A hundred dollars is a hundred dollars, that's what I say. Shoot, Angie and I got over it real quick—as soon as those bills touched our palms! We were just so happy to win *anything*!

"What are you gonna do with your share?" Angie asks Chanel.

I frown at Angie. She should know better than to ask her such a nosy question. I'll bet Miss Shopaholic has already spent her share.

"I . . . I paid back my mother with the money," Chanel whispers sadly.

"Well, that's real good, Chanel," I say, genuinely surprised. I know how much she must be hurting to part with all that money. I feel terrible for thinking badly of her before, so I put my arm around her shoulder and give her a hug.

"*Sí, mamacita,*" Chanel says, "but you're getting to go home, while we have to stay here and freeze to death or die from boredom, whichever one happens first."

"I'm not going to lie, it'll be nice to go home," Angie sighs.

"And you get to go to the Karma's Children benefit concert, too!" Chanel laments. "I wish I could go. They're *tan coolio!*"

"Yeah, well, I don't think *we're* going—even if half of Houston is," I huff.

Karma's Children may be the biggest singing group in Houston, but I don't have to *like* them. Ever since Angie and I were little girls, singing in the church choir, it was always, "Someday they'll be as good as those Karma girls."

They are older than we are, from the same neighborhood, and definitely our nemesis— they're big time, and we aren't, 'cuz they've got a record deal—*and we don't!*

"That's all anybody is talking about back home—Karma's Children, Karma's Children— I'm so *sick* of those girls!" Angie says, trying to stick a finger in my eggnog to "test" it.

"You're just green with Gucci envy, both of you," Dorinda says, breaking into a sly little smile.

"I guess so." I have to admit it, 'cuz it's true—we *are* jealous. And we'll *stay* jealous, until Def Duck records finally calls us back and tells us the Cheetah Girls have got themselves a record deal!

The doorbell rings, and Angie goes to open the front door. Galleria is finally here with her father.

"Hi, *cara, cara,* and *cara!*" Mr. Garibaldi says, greeting us with hugs and kisses. He is such a sunny personality—he always makes us smile.

Meanwhile, Galleria waltzes into the kitchen and plunks her cheetah backpack down on the linoleum floor. She looks upset.

"*Aquanetta*—when are you going home?" Mr. Garibaldi asks, hovering in the doorway. He always puts an extra "a" at the end of my name, making it sound soooo beautiful.

"I'm gonna name my eggnog 'Aquanetta-does-it-betta Eggnog' in your honor, Mr. Garibaldi," I coo. Then I answer his question. "We're leaving tomorrow morning."

"*Chè pecato.* I wanted your mother to try my specialty—chocolate cannolis. I think if she takes one bite, she would fly to New York to live, no?" Mr. Garibaldi asks, grinning from ear to ear.

Then his eyes widen. "I know—tomorrow morning, I can take you to the airport and I bring the cannolis—specially made for you, no?"

I hesitate, only because I know our Daddy will have a proper fit if we agree to let Mr. Garibaldi drive us to the airport.

Angie knows it too, because she pipes right up. "Our father is driving us, but that is so sweet of you, Mr. Garibaldi."

"Call me Franco, please, *cara Anginetta*. I come by in the morning anyway, and bring them for you." I open my mouth to say he doesn't have to, but Mr. Garibaldi shoos the words away.

"Won't you have some eggnog?" I say, trying to tempt him. "I've outdone myself again!"

"Okay, *va bene*. I've been charmed once again by the Cheetah Girls," Mr. Garibaldi says, sitting down.

Suddenly, Galleria blurts out what's on her mind. "You are not going to believe what happened. Nona was supposed to arrive on Flight #77, but the airlines from Italy are on strike."

Mr. Garibaldi comes to his daughter's aid real quick. "I tell you a funny story. When I was a young boy, I cut school one day so I could go to Lake Como just to see a girl I like." Mr. Garibaldi sips my eggnog. "Hmm, this is *perfecto*," he says, and I blush with pride.

"So I go to see this boot-i-ful girl—her name, by the way is *Pianga*, which means 'to cry' in Italian—so I should have known. My mother thinks that I'm going to school, and I tell her we have soccer practice afterward, so I will be home late. No problem. Well, when I'm ready to leave Lake Como and sneak back home to Bologna, the train is on strike! *Scioporro!* I cannot believe it!" Mr. Garibaldi moves his left hand like he is shaking flour off chicken drumsticks before frying them.

"You got in trouble?" Dorinda asks.

"I cannot tell you how much trouble," Mr. Garibaldi says, shaking his head, "all because on that day the train workers decide to strike and ruin my life!"

"How did you get home?" Dorinda asks fascinated.

"I come back to Bologna the next morning—but believe me, when I saw my father's face, I wish the strike never ended!"

Galleria is unfazed by her father's story. You

can see the disappointment on her face, even though I know Mr. Garibaldi is trying to make her feel better.

"I know, *cara*, how much you wanted to see Nona and Zia Donatella," he says, giving her a hug.

"Who is Zia Donatella?" Dorinda asks, making sure to pronounce it right. She is always transfixed by family stories.

"She's my sister—Galleria's aunt," Mr. Garibaldi offers, his face beaming.

"I wanted you to meet her," Galleria says sadly. Then she looks at me and Angie and coos, "I'm gonna miss you two."

Now Dorinda slumps in *her* chair—glum as a plum.

"When are you going to perform again, Cheetah Girls?" Mr. Garibaldi asks, trying to make us all happy again.

"Your guess is as good as ours!" Dorinda quips.

"Don't you worry, the Cheetah Girls are gonna be bigger than the Spice Rack Girls—even bigger than the invention of oregano!"

We burst out laughing, then get quiet again.

"Sitting around waiting to hear from Def

Duck Records is making us a little daffy, if you know what I'm saying," Galleria moans.

"Well, *caras*, I'd better go," Mr. Garibaldi says, getting up. "I'll see you in the morning with those chocolate cannolis. And again—the eggnog was *primo—perfecto*!" He kisses Angie's and my hands, and we giggle. Then he tips his cap and leaves.

"When is *your* dad coming home?" Galleria asks us.

"Any minute now—and he's bringing the High Priestess with him," I sigh, not looking forward to her royal presence. "If you feel a strong breeze knock you off your feet, I guess that means her broomstick has landed!"

Chapter
2

A few minutes later, we hear Daddy putting his key in the door. We're glad he is finally home from work, and we give him a big hello. We know that Daddy is under a lot of pressure with his new job at the world's biggest bug spray company, S.W.A.T. They're after him to "beef up the bottom line," he says.

Walking to the kitchen to get Daddy a glass of eggnog, I chuckle to myself. Maybe some Benjamins will fall from the sky for Daddy, just like that new song Galleria and Chanel have written, called "It's Raining Benjamins."

"Daddy, wait till you taste my latest and greatest 'Aquanetta-does-it-betta Eggnog!'"

"Not for me," Daddy grumbles.

I can't believe Daddy turned down my eggnog! I know his High Priestess girlfriend must have definitely put a spell on him, 'cuz Daddy *loves* my eggnog.

Daddy plops down on his brown leather reclining chair in the living room. Chanel, Galleria, and Dorinda hightail it back to the kitchen.

Angie and I just stand there looking at each other. I know she's feeling the same thing I am—*guilty*—'cuz Daddy is spending all this money to send us back home for the Thanksgiving holidays. He even let us go to the beauty parlor yesterday to get our nails and hair done for our trip, and I know plane tickets are especially steep this time of year. All that money pressure must be the reason he's in such a bad mood. I feel like we've ruined his holidays!

Daddy shoves some tobacco into his pipe, lights it, puffs on it a second, then blurts out what's really bothering him. "I worked so hard on this account, and somebody over at Sticky Fingers got wind of my campaign before we put it out. How else can you explain their coming up with the *same* slogan I created for a flea spray—'*Flee, you hear me?*'"

"Yeah, it sure sounds to me like the devil is working overtime," Angie offers, nodding her head like she's listening to Reverend Butter give a sermon at church.

"Y'all cleaned my blender after you used it, right?" Daddy says, looking right at me and arching his eyebrow like he does. Dag on, he cares about that blender more than he does us! Just 'cuz High Priestess Abala gave it to him as a housewarming present.

Which reminds me, I'd better remind Angie that she'd better not breathe one word about the High Priestess on a broomstick to Ma, or our Thanksgiving vacation is gonna be *ruined*.

"I bet y'all have made a mess of that kitchen, too," Dad says absentmindedly. See, this is the first dinner we've actually been allowed to cook by ourselves. "I don't want y'all spending all night cleaning up—'cuz I know you haven't packed yet."

"No, Daddy, we haven't," I mutter. How could we pack, when it took us all afternoon just to fix dinner? We had to go to school, then come home and run to Piggly Wiggly

Supermarket and buy the food, then prepare it. How could Daddy ask us such a question—and with our friends in the other room? He can be so mean sometimes!

"Don't worry, we'll get everything done in time," I assure him.

"What did y'all make for dinner, anyway?" Daddy asks, his eyes brightening a little. I think he just needed to air all that bug-spray drama to people who care about him.

"Well, let's see," I begin, "we made some honey-glazed turkey legs, collard greens with ham hocks, macaroni and cheese—"

"Blackened catfish with swamp rice," Angie chimes in.

"And gravy!" I add.

"Well, that sounds real good, girls. Y'all go ahead and enjoy yourselves with your friends." Daddy looks down at his newspaper like we're dismissed.

I look at Angie like, "Can you believe him?" I thought for sure Daddy would at least sit down to dinner with us—seeing as how we cooked it ourselves.

Looking up and seeing us still standing there, Daddy softens. "Now, you know Abala is coming over, and we're going to drink her special shakes together. Go on—can't you see how much healthier I'm looking just from drinking her shakes?" Daddy moves his eyes down to his stomach to make his point.

Yes, he has lost some weight, I think, but what if he starts disappearing before our eyes?

Like Big Momma says, though—"One monkey don't stop the show." If she ever met the Cheetah Girls, she would really get a chuckle at how true that saying is. No sooner do we sit down at the dining room table than Dorinda dives into the food like a hungry cub who hasn't eaten in days—and so do the rest of us! Later for Daddy and Abala Shaballa! *We* are going to eat this dinner, and have ourselves a good time!

Sucking the bones out of the catfish, I warn my friends, "Y'all be careful and leave the bones alone." Suddenly, I'm stricken with holiday sadness. I wish Big Momma and Ma could meet the Cheetah Girls. Going home would be so much more fun with them there. Digging into the collard greens, I know better than to say anything. I mean, it wouldn't take much to turn this crowd into an even glummer bunch!

"Good evening, good evening, ladies!"

I turn my head to see the "Holy One" waltzing into the dining room, wearing yet another of her scary creations. I mean, the wrap on her head alone is so high, it looks like it could anchor a catfish boat!

And what is that—a whole row of *teeth* around her neck? Suddenly, I realize I'm staring. Catching my manners, I blurt out, "Hi, um, High Priestess. You look nice!"

"Why, thank you, blessed one, um . . ."

Angie breaks out in a smirk, and so do I. I guess we like seeing her squirm, because she still can't tell us apart. (Angie has a beauty mark on her left cheek and I don't—but we're not going to tell her that!)

"I'm Aquanette," I say, finally coming to Abala's rescue.

"Why, yes, of course," she says, as her whole kooky coven of friends files into the dining room area. They sort of stand around like they're uncomfortable, except for the bald-headed one carrying a wicker basket full of strange vegetables I've never seen before. I can't for the life of me remember her name. . . .

"I hope you Cheetah Girls save some room

for our brew," says Abala Shaballa. "We've brought special ingredients just for you."

"Well, we're really kinda full. . . ." Galleria says, looking around at all of us for backup.

"Yes, ma'am, I don't think we're gonna be able to drink any brew tonight," I say, speaking for the rest of us.

The High Priestess looks like Chicken Little when the ceiling fell on her—I mean, she really looks panicked! "I—I was really counting on you girls participating in our ritual tonight," she stutters.

"I know, but I'm sorry—this is our last night together before we have to go home to Houston," I explain, feeling kind of bad for her.

Daddy can drink all of the strange brews he wants, but we are not going to be a part of this hocus-pocus any longer!

"Could you excuse us for a minute?" Abala Shaballa says, regaining her queenlike composure. She scurries into the living room with her coven behind her, and we can hear them whispering among themselves.

"What are y'all whispering about?" we hear Daddy asking them. But we decide not to worry ourselves with Daddy and his strange new friends. After all, this is the Cheetah Girls' last night together in New York for a whole week—and we have plenty to growl about, believe me!

Chapter 3

True to his word, the next morning Mr.
Garibaldi drops off a box of chocolate cannolis for us to take back home. Daddy puts the
cannolis on the dining room table, and yells for
us to clean our room before we go to the airport.

The way Daddy has been acting, I'm worried
that Porgy and Bess, our cherished pet guinea
pigs, are gonna be sliced up and put in some
Priestess-Pocus magic brew, instead of being
fed and loved the way they deserve. Angie and
I just don't trust Abala Shaballa—especially not
with our pets!

"I've got a great idea," I say, my eyes lighting
up. "Why don't we just bring Porgy and Bess
with us?"

Angie puts her hand over her mouth and starts to giggle.

"I know we could get in trouble, but I'm sorry—I cannot bear the thought of losing Porgy or Bess! Now, you've gotta distract Daddy," I tell Angie. In my mind, I'm already planning how we're gonna pull off Operation: Save Porgy and Bess.

"We should call Galleria," Angie says, chuckling, even though we've got to be downstairs in five minutes so Daddy can drive us to the airport. But Angie is right—if there is anybody who can pull off a mission impossible, it's Miss Galleria. That's what we like about her best—she's got growl power, as she calls it, and she's not a show-off. (Well, not exactly!)

"Come on, help me think of a plan, 'cuz we've gotta get this rodeo on the road," I whine.

Even though it's only nine o'clock and our flight to Houston is at noon, you have to check in at the airport two hours before departure—even for domestic flights! What that means is a whole lot of sitting around in the airport terminal for nothing.

"Why don't we hide the cage in Daddy's

bedroom, then yell for him to come help us with the luggage?" Angie says.

"Yeah—then you show Daddy your math homework or something, and ask his advice. While you keep him busy, I'll bring the cage down and stick it in the van! I'll get a towel from the bathroom, too."

"What's the towel for?"

"To cover the cage," I reply. Sometimes I have to spell things out for my sister.

I shove Porgy and Bess's cage into a corner of Daddy's bedroom. That's when I notice a few bottles on his nightstand. I know I'm not supposed to be in Daddy's room, but I walk over and pick up one of the bottles anyway.

I read the label. Fenugreek? *What on earth is this*? I feel a chill inside me. I open the lid of the jar and smell it: kinda like some of the herbs Big Momma uses for cooking. I run into our bedroom, and drag Angie back into Daddy's with me.

"I bet you he got these bottles from Abala Shaballa," Angie says.

"We *know* that—but what are they for?" I whisper.

Angie just shrugs her shoulders, and I can

tell she's getting as concerned about Daddy as I am. "He never even used to take an aspirin or anything—now he's running a spice shop in his bedroom!" I say, shaking my head.

Because Big Ben is ticking, Angie hightails it back to our bedroom and calls for Daddy to come help us with our suitcases. Once he's in there with Angie, I creep down the spiral staircase—which is really steep and narrow, so I have to be really careful carrying the cage.

After I put Porgy and Bess in the van and cover them, I run back inside to the refrigerator to pack a shopping bag of leftover food for our trip. I go back out to the van, place the big brown shopping bag in front of the cage, then check to see if it keeps the cage out of view. It seems Operation: Save Porgy and Bess is ready for Freddy!

When I go back inside, Daddy says to me, "Make sure to take along all that food you cooked."

"I already did," I say, happy I beat him to it. "I left you some, though."

"No need to," Daddy grunts. "You'd better take it all, because I'm not gonna eat it."

I feel the sting in my chest. "Daddy, are you

sure you're getting enough nutrients from those shakes in the blender?"

"Aquanette, I'm your Daddy, so I know what I'm doing, okay? I can't even believe I used to eat all that junk."

Junk? I know God made turkey legs and gravy for a reason!

"Abala gave me herbal supplements to take at bedtime—so don't you girls worry about me. I'm getting all the vitamins and minerals I need." Daddy smiles serenely at us.

"Okay, I'll just pack up the rest of the food," I say. Fine, if he wants it that way. The more bags in front of Porgy and Bess's cage, the better!

When we get into the van and drive off, I give Angie a meaningful look that says we were right to bring Porgy and Bess with us to Houston. Daddy didn't say one word about taking care of them, and didn't even notice they were missing!

To go to Houston from New York City, you have to fly out of LaGuardia Airport, as opposed to JFK, like we did when we went to Hollywood—the most fun experience of our lives, for sure. Suddenly, I think about the Cheetah Girls.

"A whole week without Galleria, Chanel, and Dorinda," I mumble to Angie, who is sitting next to me in the back of the van.

"I'm gonna miss them," Angie says, sad as she can be. "I feel bad for Dorinda and Chanel especially—'cuz they didn't seem like they wanted to spend Thanksgiving at home. I wish we could have invited them to come with us."

Daddy is lost in his own thoughts, but he hears the tail end of our conversation. "When are you girls gonna perform again?" he asks.

"We sure don't know," I groan. "It just seems like we can't get a break—sitting around waiting for some record company to tell us what to do. It just seems like *forever*."

"Well, on a happier note, we got here in record time," Dad says, smiling as we pull up to the Ready Rabbit Airlines entrance at the airport.

I am so furious. He's acting like he didn't even hear what I said! I heave a big sigh. That's just the way Daddy is, I tell myself.

I look at my watch. It's 9:30. It only took us twenty-five minutes to get here! Now we're gonna have to wait around for two and a half hours! "That was quick," I say, sure that Daddy won't notice the sarcastic tone in my voice either.

Before we get out of the Bronco, he turns to us and says, "Let me give you girls some extra money," then hands us each a twenty-dollar bill.

"Thank you, Daddy!" I exclaim, tears coming to my eyes. I suddenly feel terrible again, for thinking such bad things about a person when he doesn't deserve it. I've gotta stop doing that, and Angie too!

I realize now that we've been stupid and self-ish, sneaking Porgy and Bess out of the house. Daddy is gonna be piping hot when he finds out, too.

"You sure twenty dollars is enough money?" he asks, concerned.

"We haven't spent one penny of our prize money yet," Angie says proudly. That reminds me that poor Chanel had to give her money to her mother to pay off her credit card debt. Now I feel bad for her *and* Daddy.

With him being so nice, suddenly I lose my resolve for Operation: Save Porgy and Bess.

"Daddy, we wanted to bring the guinea pigs with us to Houston. Is that okay?"

"What? Now why do you want to do that?" he asks, getting that mean tone in his voice.

"Because, um, we'd miss them." It seems I've suddenly lost my resolve to tell Daddy the truth. I know if anyone disses Abala Shaballa in front of him, he loses it completely.

"Well, they're home, right where they belong. They'll be fine," Daddy says sternly, like he has dismissed me.

Angie is as quiet as a church mouse. Dag on, she's never any help when I need her!

A Ready Rabbit porter comes over to help us with our luggage. "That's okay," Daddy says to him briskly. Daddy doesn't like anybody helping him with anything.

I feel my heart pounding. Now is as good a time as any to tell Daddy the truth. "Daddy— Porgy and Bess are in the back with our luggage."

When Daddy gets mad, he breathes more fire than Puff the Magic Dragon! Without saying a word, he takes our luggage out of the van, then grabs the two shopping bags of leftover food— almost spilling the collard greens on the ground.

"I'll get it!" Angie says, like a little scaredy-cat, running after the plastic container that is rolling away down the sidewalk.

"I'm raising two daughters without their mother's help—I can certainly take care of a pair of *guinea pigs*," Daddy says, emphasizing the words like he was talking about a bunch of rodents he had to kill with S.W.A.T. Flea Spray!

"I'm sorry, Daddy," I say, tears coming to my eyes. I look over and see that Angie is about to cry, too.

Daddy frowns, then sighs. "Ah, go ahead and take them with you," he says, putting the cage on the luggage cart and pushing it inside. "Let them be your headache, not mine."

Well, we're just fine with that. Fine, that is, until a Ready Rabbit Airlines representative comes up to Daddy and says, "That will be seventy-five dollars for the pets, sir."

"Oh, I won't be paying for it," Daddy says. "*They* will." he says, pointing to us.

The representative turns to Angie and me. "If you plan on bringing your pets on board, ladies, you'll have to pay an additional seventy-five dollars."

I almost start stuttering, I'm so upset. "I'll pay it," Angie says, whipping out her wallet.

I can feel Daddy's gaze on us, but I'm too

scared to look at him. I reach into my backpack and take out my bottle of air-sickness pills. I'm already feeling airsick, and we're not even off the ground yet.

I hand one to Angie, too, and she pops it into her mouth. Last month, when we flew to Hollywood with the Cheetah Girls, Angie and I were so excited we forgot to take our pills. We ended up throwing up *everything*. It was so embarrassing!

"Bye, Daddy," Angie says, after she's parted with most of *her* prize money and we've been checked in. Bye, Daddy, is right. And bye, prize money, too.

When we finally reach Porgy and Bess's storage space, which is almost at the tail of the plane, I set the cage down on its rack. "I hope you two enjoy the ride—'cuz it sure cost enough," I tell them.

"I bet *our* tickets cost a whole lot more than seventy-five dollars," Angie reminds me as we walk back to our seats in the middle of the plane. "Come on, let's forget about it. We still have some spending money left. Let's just pray that Galleria, Chanel, and Dorinda have a blessed Thanksgiving."

We sit down, buckle up, and Angie takes my hand. Like we do every time we fly, we hold hands now, and say a prayer until the plane takes off.

When we're finally airborne, and we can see the big, white fluffy clouds that look just like cotton balls, we let go of each other's hands and breathe a deep sigh of relief.

Hot sauce, Houston, and Karma's Children, here we come!

Chapter 4

I never thought I'd be so happy just to walk through a busy airport terminal—but that's exactly the exhilaration I feel when we hit George Bush Intercontinental after our six-hour journey, which included a layover in Chicago, where we caught our connecting flight to Houston.

"Hi, Ma!" Angie screeches, throwing her arms around our mother like she's been lost at sea, and Ma's a lifesaver.

Meanwhile, Ma is peeking over Angie's shoulder at Porgy and Bess in their cage.

"What on earth?" Ma mumbles, her eyes twinkling because she knows we are up to something.

"Um . . ." I hesitate when Angie looks at me.

We have to be *very* careful what we tell Ma. Angie and I have decided we are not going to tell her about Daddy's kookiness—drinking concoctions out of the blender and such—and definitely not one word about his new girl-friend Abala, not even if Ma spoon-feeds us turnips for forty straight hours to force a con-fession out of us!

"Um—we've never been away from Porgy and Bess for a whole week, and we don't want them getting lonely," I say.

"Your father let you bring them down here?" Ma asks, her eyes bright with disbelief.

"Well, we had to pay an extra seventy-five dollars and the flight attendant didn't even serve them lunch!" Angie moans.

"If we'd have known about that, Porgy and Bess would still be home, munching on their carrots!" I quickly add.

Laughing, Ma grabs the handle of the cage and puts it on the luggage cart. She looks smaller than I remember her. At first I think it must be because Angie and I have gotten taller. But then, looking down at her feet, I realize it's probably because she isn't wearing high heels.

I wonder why not. Ma always wears high

heels with her pantsuits, and she is wearing a pantsuit today—this one is powder blue with a pretty (fake) flower in the lapel of the jacket.

"You look nice," I tell Ma, giving her a hug, and savoring the sweet scent of her Shalimar cologne. I sure miss that smell.

"Thank you, 'Nettie One,'" Mom says, stroking some misplaced strands on my bob into place. (That's Mom's nickname for me. Angie's is "Nettie Two." I guess it's because I was born first—by five minutes.)

"I don't know where your Uncle Skeeter is, but he was supposed to come to the airport with me to pick you girls up," Ma adds, a flicker of darkness passing through her warm, brown eyes.

I feel a twinge of disappointment, but I try to hide it. I love my uncle Skeeter, and I just assumed he would come with Ma to meet us. Uncle Skeeter is Ma's younger brother—and a whole lot of fun.

"How was your flight?" Ma asks, regaining her sweet composure.

"Everybody loved our corn bread!" I tell her, breaking out into a big grin.

"We made dinner all by ourselves, for our

friends the Cheetah Girls," Angie explains. "And we thought we'd bring you the leftovers. But you know how bad airline food is. Well, Angie and I ended up feeding half the passengers!"

"Angie is exaggerating, of course," I say. "We only fed about *fifty*." I chuckle as I hand Ma the last container of potato salad, which we saved just for her. "Tell us what you think—it's not as good as Big Momma's, but I think you'll like it. Our friends loved it."

"I'll bet they did," Ma says with a big smile. "Thank you, sweeties."

"Oh—here are some chocolate cannolis Mr. Garibaldi made for us," Angie says, handing Ma the box.

"Who is Mr. Gari-body?"

"He's Bubbles's father—you know, Galleria from the Cheetah Girls," Angie says, acting kinda "bubbly" herself.

"We wish you could meet our friends. You'll love the Cheetah Girls!" I add.

"Well, I love these outfits—you picked these out yourselves?" Ma asks, curious.

"No, remember we told you about Ms. Dorothea—that's Bubble's mom, and she's now our manager, too. Well, she made them for us after we performed at the Apollo Theatre. They were supposed to be a victory gift, but you know—we lost. So she surprised us with them anyway."

"Well, they are beautiful," Ma says, but there is a tinge of something sad in her voice. Suddenly I feel guilty about being so close with Ms. Dorothea. 'Course, I know that's silly, because Ma wants the best for us, even if she can't be there to share in all the good and bad times.

We all get real quiet for a second, and that's when I notice Ma's nails. The polish on them is chipped—which is strange, because she always keeps her nails nice. I can tell Ma's still thinking—probably about Ms. Dorothea making us outfits and doing stuff for us. I can tell she feels sad about *something*.

We drive onto the Southwest Freeway to get to our house in Sugar Land, which is a suburb in southwest Houston. Mom has put on her dark Gucci sunglasses, and her permed hair is blowing like feathers fluttering in the wind.

"You just washed the car?" I ask her, admiring the spanking-clean upholstery.

"Yes, indeed," she says, taking a deep sigh. "You girls got any concerts coming up?"

Dag on, why does everybody ask us that? You'd think we were Karma's Children or something—touring around the world, and only coming back home to Houston for some corn bread and bedtime stories when we got exhausted from all that fame and fortune!

"No, we don't," I respond.

"Well, when are you gonna start recording for the record company—what's it called again, Daffy Duck?"

"No. It's called Def Duck Records, Ma—but they might as well be 'Daffy,' 'cuz we sure haven't heard anything yet," I huff. "Ms. Dorothea says we just have to sit tight."

Ma gets real quiet again. Why is it every time I mention Ms. Dorothea's name, she seems to get upset?

There *is* something different about Ma. Maybe it's just because we haven't seen her since June. That's when we moved to New York, after a whole lot of hushed phone conversations and long-distance screaming. Personally, I think CIA negotiations for hostages went smoother than our parents' dee-vorce. Oh, well—at least now that it's over, Daddy and Ma are polite and civil to each other on the phone.

"Big Momma is expecting us at her house, but I told her y'all probably wanted to hang out at home for a little while first," Ma says.

"I know Big Momma can't wait to see us, but we do need a bubble bath!" Angie chuckles.

"You know how Big Momma is. She wants to see her 'babies.' Egyptian and India are waiting for y'all too."

Egyptian and India are our cousins—Uncle Skeeter's children from his first marriage. They spend a lot of time over at Big Momma's now that their father is living there. Uncle Skeeter is a grown man, but Ma says he seems to have fallen on hard times. That's why he moved back into Big Momma's house.

"Wait till y'all see the outfit Skeeter put together for the Karma's Children benefit," Ma says, chuckling. She doesn't realize that she has just opened up an old wound for me and Angie. "He went to Born-Again Threads and bought himself some metallic purple bell-bottoms, and an even more ridiculous fedora—oh, and a red fake-fur jacket—"

"Ma!" Angie says, chiding her.

"Don't 'Ma' me—just wait till you see Mr. Disco! I told him just because it's a benefit for the homeless, doesn't mean he has to *look* homeless!"

Angie puts her hand over her mouth and giggles. She can pretend she isn't jealous of Karma's Children all she wants. I *know* she is *just* as jealous as I am.

"I don't know if we're gonna go to the benefit," I blurt out.

"Why not?" Ma asks, looking at me in the rearview mirror. "I told you, I'll pay for the tickets."

The tickets for the Karma's Children benefit concert are fifty dollars each. All the money is going to the Montgomery Homeless Shelter, which is in the worst part of Houston.

Ma is still waiting for an answer, but then she figures it out all by herself. "Don't tell me y'all are jealous of those girls, just 'cuz they're famous now. You used to *love* them. I 'member that time when nobody knew who they were, and y'all wanted to go see them at the Crabcake Lounge. You cried for two days 'cuz I wouldn't let you go!"

"We were nine years old—that was a long time ago!" I grumble. "They aren't any more talented than we are. Why should we go see *them* perform?"

"You should be happy they're doing well—that means *you* have a chance, too," Ma says, in that tone of voice she uses when she's giving us a lecture.

We all get quiet, for what seems like hours. Then Angie asks Ma, "Do you think Big Momma will mind if we bring Porgy and Bess over to her house, so they can run around in her garden?"

"I don't know—you'd better call and ask her first," Ma says hesitantly.

"Ooo, wait till they get a hold of her strawberries!" Angie says, snickering.

"Big Momma will have you in that garden on your hands and knees replanting fruits and vegetables till you're ninety, if you don't watch out," Ma warns us.

She pulls her Katmobile into our four-car garage, and it finally hits me: *We iz home!*

Once we've hauled all our things inside, I ask, "Ma, is it okay if we call Galleria and tell her we made it here?"

"Who's Galleria again?" Ma asks absentmindedly, clearing some plates off the dining room table.

I can't believe my eyes. This place is a *mess*. If we had left the house like this, she would have grounded Angie and me for the rest of our lives!

"*Galleria Garibaldi*. She's the leader of the Cheetah Girls—our singing group," I say in a sarcastic tone, since Ma obviously doesn't remember things that are important to *us*.

"Oh, I don't think you ever told me her name," Ma says.

"Her mother, Ms. Dorothea, named her after the Galleria mall here in Houston—ain't that funny?" Angie says, trying to be helpful like always, even though Ma isn't really listening. "See, Ms. Dorothea was here in Houston working—I think she was modeling for some catalogue—and she was pregnant. She went shopping at the Galleria and bought her first pair of Gucci shoes, so that's why she named her daughter Galleria."

"Lucky for her she could afford Gucci shoes," Ma says firmly. "When your father and I were raising you, by the time we finished paying for everything, I was lucky to be able to get a pair of Payless pumps."

Finally, Angie gets the message. Meanwhile,

I have dialed Galleria's bedroom phone, and luckily she's there. "We're home!" I say, trying to sound chirpy.

"That's good," Galleria says, sniffling.

"What's wrong, Bubbles?" Now Angie is hovering by me, trying to hear the phone conversation.

"Nona is not coming after all! She went to Turin for a mud bath, and she slipped and broke her hip. Daddy is flying over there to be with her, but Ma's working, so we're *stuck* here!"

"Oh no, I can't believe it!" I say, trying to console her. "Angie and I are gonna say a prayer for you."

"We're gonna say one for you, too," Galleria says.

Ma throws me a look. "You two better start getting ready."

"Yes, ma'am," I say without thinking. I can feel tears welling up in my eyes. That's the first time Galleria has ever said anything about praying. She always used to make fun of Angie and me with our church stuff.

You know what? God really *does* work in mysterious ways. . . .

Chapter 5

If there is one thing we miss about Houston, it's taking a bite out of Big Momma's peach cobbler! Well, finally our long wait is over. Stepping out of Ma's car as we pull up in front of Big Momma's house, I notice that some of the kids hanging out down the block stop to stare at us. This one boy, with red kinky hair and freckles, starts walking toward us, waving.

"Who is that?" Angie asks.

"I don't know," I respond, watching him and thinking how much faster he could walk if he tied his sneaker laces.

"What, y'all moved up to the Big Apple and forgot about us?" the redheaded boy screeches as he approaches.

"It's Beethead!" Angie whispers.

It sure is—even though his hair is not as bushy. Major "Beethead" Knowles is the reason why I have seven stitches in my left knee and don't like wearing skirts. When I was about four years old, I was swinging real high, showing off, of course. Beethead kept throwing rocks at me, to see if he could reach my head. He did, causing me to fall off the swing and bust my knee on a jagged rock edge. Big Momma told Beethead never to come anywhere near us again. And he hasn't—until now.

"Hey, Beethead," I exclaim, and he breaks out in a grin.

"Check y'all out," he says, examining our cheetah outfits. "Y'all sure look *different*."

The other kids are still staring at us, too—like we're in a zoo or something. I guess we're gonna cause quite a stir in Houston with our new "cheetah-ness."

"I'll see y'all inside," Ma yells as she walks up to the front of Big Momma's house. Beethead waves at Ma, and she waves back, smiling.

"Y'all got tickets yet to the Karma's Children's concert?"

"No, we haven't," I reply.

"Well, you better get 'em soon, 'cuz they're almost sold out," Beethead says, trying to be helpful.

"Well—we'll see," I respond, without further explanation.

Beethead props himself against the big oak tree outside Big Momma's house. I never noticed that he had such long eyelashes before—almost like a girl's.

"What's that?" Beethead says, pointing at Porgy and Bess's cage.

"That's our guinea pigs," I reply.

Beethead heckles so loud, I almost expect him to expose hyena fangs any minute. Ugh. Now I don't think he's cute *at all*.

We say good-bye to the heckling Beethead, and go up the front steps. Angie chuckles, and says, "He sure got skinnier."

"He sure did," I say, then coo at Porgy and Bess. "That's okay if Beethead doesn't like y'all. I'll bet Big Momma's gonna *love* you."

Big Momma never did have the pleasure of meeting Porgy and Bess when we lived at home, because she never came upstairs to our bedroom. These last few years, she has slowed down quite a bit, and she uses a cane to get around.

"Look at y'all!" Big Momma says, standing still in the doorway so she can get a look at us. She peers closely at my cheek—I guess to see if there's a beauty mark.

"It's Aquanette, Big Momma," I say, helping her out.

"I know how to tell my grandchildren apart, Nettie One," she says, shooing me with her hand. "My, my, my—those are quite some get-ups y'all got on!"

"This is what we wear when we're the Cheetah Girls!" Angie exclaims, and we pose so Big Momma can admire us.

"Don't just stand there, take off your coats—the pawnshop's closed!" Big Momma says, chuckling at her own joke.

I set Porgy and Bess's cage down, and hug Big Momma real tight. Then she hugs Angie. Our cousins Egyptian and India come running into the foyer. Egyptian is ten and India is almost eight, but she is the same height as her older sister.

"We're so glad y'all finally got here—now we can eat!" India says sassily. She has big bug eyes, just like Uncle Skeeter, but her demeanor is more like her mother's—Aunt Neffie—high and mighty.

Personally, I don't think Aunt Neffie's name is really Nefertiti like she claims, even though Ma says that now she sure is a queen, "sitting alone on a throne." (She means because Aunt Neffie and Uncle Skeeter got separated.)

"Is Uncle John coming?" Egyptian asks me, even though she knows Daddy moved to New York because he and Ma got dee-vorced.

"No. Is Aunt Neffie here?" I ask, playing the same game. Aunt Neffie doesn't come to Big Momma's now that Uncle Skeeter is living back home.

"Oooo!" India says, eyeing Porgy and Bess in the cage.

Now Big Momma sees them too, and grunts, "Guess there ain't much bacon under those hides. Not worth cookin'."

"Big Momma!" I squeal, then grab her waist. She's just joking, though. Big Momma wouldn't hurt a fly.

"Can we take them out to the garden?" India asks, picking up Porgy and Bess's cage.

"That's where they belong," Big Momma says, smiling.

"Why didn't Skeeter meet me to go to the airport?" Ma asks Big Momma as she helps her put the "good" silverware on the table. (Big Momma always puts out the good stuff when company comes.)

"I don't know," Big Momma says, distracted. "I think it's time to get the corn bread out of the oven."

She hobbles over to it, and Ma runs to help her. "Sit down now—I'll take care of everything."

Egyptian cuts me a look and tries to mouth something to me, but I can't understand what she's saying. I put my finger up to my mouth and tell her to "shhh" and tell me later.

"Big Momma, how was the Quilt Festival this year?" I ask quickly, so she doesn't know we were whispering. Even though she's slowed down some, Big Momma wouldn't miss the Quilt Festival for anything.

"Junie—how many quilts did they have there this year?" Big Momma turns and asks Ma.

"I think more than nine hundred," Ma calls out.

"They sure were beautiful," Big Momma says.

Egyptian starts mouthing at me again. I shake my head at her and tell her to stop. She probably is trying to give me a blow-by-blow account of one of Aunt Neffie and Uncle Skeeter's battles.

Angie and I feel bad for Egyptian and India because they're younger than we are, and it's hard for them to understand that sometimes grown-ups are better off separating than staying together and being miserable.

"Are y'all gonna go down to Kemah's Boardwalk to audition?" Egyptian asks nonchalantly, dabbing pink lip gloss on her lips from a Glitter Gurlie tube, like she's grown.

"What audition are you talking about?" I respond, not looking up because I'm trying to get a napkin into the holder just right, so the fan shape is perfect.

"You know—they're looking for unknown groups for the Karma's Children benefit concert. Didn't Aunt Junie tell you?" Egyptian licks her lips again, then jumps up to get Ma's attention. "Aunt Junie, didn't you tell Nettie One and Two about the poster up in the Galleria?"

"What poster are you talking about?" Ma shoots back.

"Aunt Junie—you'd have to be blind to miss it. It's got their picture on it and everything," Egyptian says, exasperated.

"Whose picture?" Angie asks.

"Karma's Children!" Egyptian says, like we're all stupid.

"They've even got on outfits like y'all's," India says, grinning straight at me, even though her left eye isn't. India has a wandering eye, which is probably why she is nicer than her sister. Kids have been making fun of her eyes ever since she could talk, and I think getting made fun of makes a person more sensitive.

"No, they don't," Egyptian says, cutting off her sister. "They're polka dots, stupid!"

"Well, they look the same," India says, shrugging. She pours some of the beads and crystals out of the pinto beans can she uses to store all her arts and crafts stuff.

"Don't do that now! Big Momma will get mad!" Egyptian hisses, picking up the beads, some of which have rolled onto the floor. "Now look what you've done!"

Ma comes out of the kitchen with a serving

pan of corn bread, and puts it on the table. "What poster are you talking about, 'Gyptian?" she asks.

"They are looking for unknown groups to open for Karma's Children for the benefit concert at Kemah's," Egyptian says, like she is so-o tired of repeating herself.

"'Gyptian, how am I going to tell them about a poster I never saw?" Ma shoots back.

"*Everybody* is talking about it," Egyptian counters. "It's right outside the Glitter Gurlie store in the Galleria. Even people who can't sing are gonna audition for it!"

"'Gyptian, I haven't been to the Glitter Gurlie store, now have I? But it's obvious *you* have," Ma says disapprovingly, first looking at the tube of lip gloss in Egyptian's hands, then at the glittery gunk she has smeared on her lips.

Egyptian puts her head down meekly, toying with the lip gloss tube in her hand.

"Now, you know you'd better go wash that stuff off before Big Momma sees it," Ma says sternly.

"India, exactly what does the poster say?" I ask my younger cousin, since she's more level-headed than her sister.

"They're having auditions tomorrow for unknown groups who want to sing at the Karma's Children concert," India says.

"That's what it said, huh?" I respond. The wheels in my head are turning faster than on a Bronco.

"'Help Us Sing for Their Supper,'" Egyptian adds nonchalantly. "That's what it says at the top of the poster."

"I wonder if they're paying," I mutter out loud.

"Who cares?" Ma shoots back. "It sounds like it could be the opportunity of a lifetime!"

"Well, we've sure heard *that* one before," I chuckle, and look at Angie.

"We'd better get down to the mall tomorrow morning and look at the sign," Angie says, ignoring me.

"You don't have to," India says.

"Why not?" I ask.

"'Cuz I wrote down the number for myself!" she answers proudly. Then she sees Egyptian glaring at her, so she stutters, "'Gyptian and I just want to meet Karma's Children and get an autograph."

"I didn't see you write down any number," Egyptian hisses.

"I did it when you went inside the store!" India says adamantly, pulling out a paper from her purse. "Here it is!"

I take the paper from India and run to the phone. "Let me hear!" Angie insists, as I dial the number and wait.

"It's just ringing!" I hiss back. A recorded message comes on, and I tilt the phone receiver so Angie can hear it too:

"We care about Houston. Do you? If you want to help out Houston's homeless, then make a date with stardom. Unknown groups can audition for the Karma's Children benefit concert on November 23rd, at The Crabcake Lounge, Kemah's Boardwalk in Galveston Bay. If you're a singing group in the Houston area, this may be your chance to shine. Auditions will be held on November 21st from 10 A.M. to 4 P.M. Come help Houston's hottest stars sing for their supper. Call 800-000-GETHOME to order your tickets now!"

Angie and I look at each other. "We have to swallow our pride and go to that audition," I confess excitedly.

Ma just looks at me, and smiles. "I'm glad to see you've come to your senses, Nettie One."

"Yes, ma'am, I am too!" I tell her. Then I turn to India and give her a big hug. "I guess if it wasn't for your divette detective skills, we wouldn't be going to any audition!" I tell her.

"You know, they only want groups from here," Angie points out.

"Yes—and?" I ask.

"What about the *rest* of the Cheetah Girls?"

"Oh," I say, finally realizing what she means. I was so busy thinking about Angie and me performing that I forgot about them. "That's right—they're from New York City. So what are we gonna do?"

Big Momma has brought out the rest of the food, and overhears the end of our deep discussion. "What's wrong?" she asks.

We explain the predicament to her while shoveling food into our mouths.

"I think y'all should go—one monkey don't stop no show," Big Momma says, giving us her familiar line of advice.

"All right," I respond, looking at Angie, who nods her head like she agrees.

"Momma, where is Skeeter?" Ma asks Big

Momma again. She's been quiet all this time, and I guess she's been worrying about her brother.

I chuckle to myself. He's probably down at Slick Willie's in Bayou Place, playing pool as usual. That's one of the reasons he and Aunt Neffie used to fight—'cuz he wasn't home half the time.

"Never mind about Skeeter, Junifred." Big Momma only calls Ma by her real name when she is irritated. I wonder why that should be. . . .

I dig into my macaroni and cheese, and a thought hits me like a can of lard upside my head: *How can we go on an audition without the Cheetah Girls?*

I look over at Angie. Like always, she knows just what I'm thinking. Big Momma is right. One monkey don't stop no show. We'll just go on the audition and see what happens. Judging by what Egyptian said, probably everybody and their mother will be there. We'll be lucky if we even *get* to audition.

We go out in the garden to play. Outside, Egyptian rushes up to me and blurts out what's been on her mind the whole time. "Daddy hasn't been home for three whole days!" she says.

"Is that right?" I gasp, alarmed.

India runs outside when she hears us out there. "We don't know where he is. He hasn't called or anything. Big Momma is worried sick—and so are we!" India looks exasperated, which seems to make her wandering eye wander even farther.

I check through the window. Ma and Big Momma are still chattering away in the living room.

"You don't know where Uncle Skeeter is?" Angie asks.

Egyptian firmly shakes her head "no."

India's eyes light up, and she says, "He has a girlfriend downtown. I heard him talking on the phone with her."

"How do you know he was talking to his girlfriend?" Egyptian asks, like she doesn't believe her sister.

"'Cuz he was giggling a lot," India says, like she knows what she's talking about.

Angie and I just smile at her. I think my cousin India really does have the makings of a "divette detective," but now is not the time to make a big fuss over her. We have more important matters at hand.

I don't like this situation one bit—especially since Big Momma is trying to cover it up. "Do you have the girlfriend's phone number?" I ask India.

"No," she says, disappointed.

"What was her name?"

"I don't know, but Daddy said into the phone, 'Girl, you are just like your name—softer than a mink coat.'" Sadness flickers in India's eyes.

"We'll find out what's going on," I assure my cousins, trying to sound hopeful. They seem so scared about their daddy having disappeared for three days, and I don't blame them one bit. I'm anxious about it myself.

"Can Porgy and Bess stay here with us one more day?" India asks, not missing a beat.

"Of course they can," I say, pleased that I'm able to give my cousins something that'll make them happy.

At the end of the evening, walking back to Ma's car, Angie mutters, "We'd better call Galleria as soon as we get home."

"Yeah—I don't feel right about this whole thing."

"You mean about Uncle Skeeter?" Angie

asks, as we lean against Ma's Katmobile, waiting for her to come outside.

"No—about going on some audition without them."

"Yeah," Angie agrees.

When Ma gets in the car, I blurt out what our cousins told us about Uncle Skeeter. "Ma, he hasn't been home for three days."

Ma lets out a sigh. "Big Momma was never good at lying—I'll tell you that," she says.

Chapter 6

When we get home, I ask Ma if we can call Galleria on the phone. I *know* it would be too much to ask if we could log on to her computer, but we're dying to talk to all of the Cheetah Girls. If there was ever a time when we needed a council meeting, it's *right now*.

"Whazzup, Houston?" Galleria cackles into the phone.

It's kinda weird telling Bubbles about our predicament—an audition that popped up outta nowhere.

"Well, the three of us can't afford to come down to Houston and tiptoe through the tulips with the two of you, Miz Aquanette," Galleria says, trying to sound like it doesn't bother her.

But I *know* Bubbles—she's usually down for anything, and always up to something, as Big Momma would say. She says good-bye with a chirp in her voice, but I can hear the sadness underneath.

"We could just end up singing in a soup kitchen, for all we know," Angie says, spritzing the dining room table with Splendid Cleaning Spray.

"Angie, don't use that!" I hiss to my absent-minded sister. She's always pulling stuff like that when she's too lazy to do something the right way. "Go get the lemon oil and a nice soft rag."

It's nine o'clock in the morning, but Ma is still upstairs sleeping, which is very unusual in itself. On top of her not wearing her high heels with her pantsuit, and her chipped nails, things are beginning to add up, and I don't like the answer I'm getting—something is wrong with our ma.

We're creeping around downstairs trying to clean, because I can't believe how messy the house is. It's just not like her—*especially* leaving cigarette butts in the ashtrays.

"Those are Uncle Skeeter's," Angie says, picking up one of the butts and seeing the "Lucky Ducky" brand on the filter. Yes, that's Uncle Skeeter's brand, all right.

Suddenly, I feel a pang in my chest. I can just see him smoking, cackling and coughing at the same time. I wonder where he could be?

"Do you think Galleria was upset?" Angie asks, spreading a few drops of lemon oil on a corner of the table and wiping it carefully with the rag like she should.

"I think Bubbles is more upset about her grandmother than anything else," I tell Angie.

"We'd better wake Ma up," Angie says with a sigh. Ma is driving us to the audition, and we'd rather go earlier than later, just to get it over with. Like I said before, who knows what we're walking into?

Just then, right on cue, Ma walks past us and plops down at the kitchen counter.

"Good morning, Sleeping Beauty," Angie says.

"I knew something was fishy when Skeeter came over the other day," Ma says. Heaving a deep sigh, she covers her face with her hands.

"When did he come over?" I ask concerned.

"Monday—no, it was last Sunday, that's right. His eyes were glassy. I could tell he'd been drinking."

Ma screws up her face like Uncle Skeeter and imitates him. "'That uptight husband of yours, John Walker, may be my brother-in-law—but Johnnie Walker Red is my *cuzzin*.'"

Johnnie Walker Red is the brand of Scotch Uncle Skeeter likes. Even Daddy keeps it in the bar at our house in New York, but he has never made one joke about having the same name as a brand of liquor. That's Daddy for you.

I walk over and give Ma a hug. I'm so glad she has stopped pretending we are too young to understand these things. We've known since we were real little that Uncle Skeeter drinks, smokes, and doesn't go to church, and that it bothers everybody in my family. We also know that Uncle Skeeter and Daddy never got along.

"What did Skeeter say when he came over?" Angie asks.

"He said he was tired of trying to make everybody happy, and just wanted to go some-where he could 'rest in peace,'" Ma says sadly. Then she chuckles, because Uncle Skeeter was probably making a joke off Granddaddy Walker's funeral parlor, Rest in Peace.

"But India says he has a new girlfriend?" Angie asks gingerly.

Ma doesn't seem at all bothered that we know. "Yeah. I don't remember her name— something Wilkerson. Skeeter said, 'That Wilkerson woman sure knows how to treat a man.' That's all I remember."

Hmmm. "India says she heard him on the phone with his girlfriend, saying something like, 'you sure are just like your name—softer than a mink coat!'"

Ma rubs her eyes and dismisses me. "What would India know? She's just a child." No sooner than the words are out of her mouth, Ma realizes what she's said, and who she's talking to. We chuckle along with her.

"Ma, what's wrong?" I ask, hoping that now that we've been so honest with each other, she won't try to cover up other things. "I mean, *besides* Uncle Skeeter being missing?"

All of a sudden, I see the tears well up in Ma's eyes, and she lets them roll down her cheeks without even wiping them. Angie and I sit real still at the table, waiting for Ma to talk.

"I don't know which is worse, living with your father and being miserable, or living without him and being so damn *lonely*," Ma says, her voice cracking. "All I do now is get up, go to work, pay bills, then get up and do it all over again. Not that I have anything to get up for now, with y'all gone."

Now I know what's bothering Ma. She *misses* us—all this time pretending she didn't mind if we lived with Daddy! Angie starts whimpering, and now I feel the tears well up in my eyes, too.

"We don't want to go on the audition," Angie says. "Let's just stay here together. I mean, what if it isn't for real?"

"Egyptian and India told you about it, right?" Ma stops her.

"Yeah," Angie replies, wiping tears from her cheeks.

"Well, then I suggest the two of you go, because those kids seem to be the only ones around here who *do* know what's going on." Ma laughs, then looks down at her raggedy nails. "Lord knows I need to do something with these claws."

Angie and I chuckle, but I know we both feel

guilty inside. *Our* hair and nails look nice, 'cuz Daddy pays for us to go to the beauty parlor twice a month in New York. But I don't think we deserve that, if Ma is miserable.

I look over at Ma, and she suddenly breaks out in a smile. It's the first time her smile has seemed genuine since we've been here. "I love y'all, you know that?" she says. "It's so good to have you back here—even if it's only for one week."

Galveston Bay is about thirty minutes by car from where we live. Ma puts the top down on her Katmobile, and Angie and I start singing "It's Raining Benjamins."

> "For the first time in her-story
> there's a weather forecast
> that looks like the mighty cash.
> So tie up your shoes and
> put away your blues
> 'cuz we're going around the bend
> at half past ten
> to the only place in town
> where everything is coming up green
> you know what I mean:

It's raining Benjamins
for a change and some coins
It's raining Benjamins
I heard that
It's raining . . . again!!!!"

Ma is bopping along with us. "Y'all sound g-o-o-d!" she shouts over the noise of the wind.

"That's what we're gonna sing for our audition," I say triumphantly.

"We are?" Angie seems surprised, even though that's the song we were rehearsing just before we left. "I guess I'm just used to us singing 'Wanna-be Stars in the Jiggy Jungle.'"

I can tell Angie is a little nervous, but that's too bad—*I've* made up *our* mind.

"We're only going to be doing two-part harmonies instead of five—it's a better song for that, Angie," I say, just wishing she would go along, just this once, without questioning things.

"Okay," she says, shrugging her shoulders. "It doesn't matter, anyway. We'll be lucky if we even get *into* this dag-on audition."

"If nothing else, we got out of the house!" Ma says chirpily. I can definitely see she is feeling much better. "Y'all sing so different than you used to in church."

"We're not in church, Ma!" I exclaim. "We can't sing the same way."

"I know, I know. Don't worry, I like it," Ma says nicely, then asks, "Who thought up that song?"

"Well—it's a long story," I say, looking over at Angie. "See, Chanel's mom—"

"Who's Chanel?" Ma asks, smiling, like she knows I'm gonna brain her if she doesn't get all these names right.

"Chanel and Galleria are best—well, I mean, oldest—friends, because their mothers were friends—"

"And big models," Angie blurts out.

"Okay, so Chanel's mom, Mrs. Simmons, she's got this boyfriend we call Mr. Tycoon— he's a sheik or something—"

"*Real* rich!" Angie chuckles, but I poke her. She knows Ma is feeling lonely, so why does she have to rub it in?

"Anyway, Mrs. Simmons is writing this book, called *It's Raining Sheiks*, about women who have sheiks for boyfriends or something."

"But not all of them are happy," Angie adds,

like she knows what she's talking about.

"Stop interrupting me," I hiss.

"Okay, I'm sorry, I'm just trying—"

"I know." I cut her off. "So, Chanel—that's our friend from the Cheetah Girls—"

"I *know* who Chanel is now," Ma says, switching on her blinker because she is about to change lanes on the freeway.

"So Chanel had this dream about money falling from the sky, and she told Galleria. But see, Chanel doesn't like it that *Galleria* writes all our songs, so she goes ahead and writes two lines for the new song—"

"Uh-uh," Angie says, holding up her hand. "She only wrote *one* line."

"Yes, you're right—bless her heart—she wrote one little line in her notebook, Galleria said. Galleria went over to Chanel's house, and *she* wrote the rest of the song—but it's cute, right?"

"Yeah, it's cute," Ma says as we approach the exit for Kemah Boardwalk, which is right on the water.

I hum some more of the song. I wish Ma could meet the Cheetah Girls, and Ms. Dorothea, and even Mr. Garibaldi. They sure know how to have fun. Ma would love them.

I know I've been running my mouth, but I've got to tell Ma the story of how Mr. and Mrs. Garibaldi met each other. I remember when we first heard the story, Angie and I thought we had just met the kookiest people in New York. Who knew they would turn out to be the happiest people we've met there so far?

"Ma—you know how Galleria's mom and dad met?" I ask.

Now Angie throws me a look like, "Why you wanna bring that up when you know Ma and Daddy are dee-vorced!" I decide maybe I'd better not tell Ma, but she eggs me on.

"Why'd you stop talking? Tell me the story," she says, amused.

"Well, they met through the *New York* magazine personals ads."

"Really?" Ma says, and now she seems real interested.

"Yes. Mr. Garibaldi's ad said, 'Lonely oyster on the half-shell seeks rare black pearl to feel complete,'" I say, laughing out loud, and even Angie joins in. I don't care how many times I hear that, it just tickles me silly. "I *saw* the ad, Ma—they have it in the family photo album!"

Ma bursts out laughing. "That is funny. Is he Eye-talian?"

"Yes, he is—and he cooks, too! Weren't those chocolate cannolis dee-licious?" I ask.

"Yes, indeed," Ma says wistfully. "Maybe that's what I need to be doing."

"Making cannolis?" Angie asks, puzzled.

"No. Answering personal ads like Ms. Gari-bodi," Ma chuckles.

"Ma—her name is Ms. Gari-baldi—and you'd better not be doing anything foolish like that!" Angie exclaims.

"I don't know how foolish it is—y'all seem to like those people, so they must be nice—'cuz I know we raised you right. But do you know what the chances are of a black woman over forty finding another man?"

"What?" Angie and I ask in unison.

"Less than the chances of getting hit by a plane falling from the sky," Ma says.

We both laugh, relieved, because Ma is obviously joking.

"You laugh? One in forty thousand—that's what it said in *Sistarella* magazine," Ma says, getting out of the car and shutting the door. "Y'all want me to go inside with you?"

That's just like Ma, changing the subject when she's talking about something serious. I'm not gonna let her off the hook that easy. "Those statistics don't say anything about a beautiful woman like you, Ma," I say, giving her a hug.

"Well, I guess your Daddy didn't think I was so beautiful."

We are stunned, so we don't say anything. We are definitely not telling Ma about Daddy's new girlfriend!

"Don't think I don't know your Daddy is up to something, either," Ma says, shoving the keys into her purse and zipping it up. "He's been awfully nice these past few months."

"Well . . ." Angie begins.

"Nettie Two, don't open your mouth before you know what's coming out of it. You never were good at lying—so don't think you've suddenly improved overnight."

I was gonna get Angie back good myself, but Ma beat me to it.

"That's all right—if I was your daddy, I'd be careful of any woman fool enough to put up with him. That's all I've got to say," Ma huffs, then looks at the thousands of people descending on the Boardwalk like locusts. "Boy, they sure have a lot of tourists here for the holidays, don't they?"

"I guess so," I mutter.

As we walk closer, we see that all the people are concentrated in one area, making it impossible for us to get by. That's when we hear the man with the bullhorn, saying, "Everyone is going to get to audition. The line will go a whole lot quicker if you stay to the left of the railing."

Ma looks at us and says, "Well, I guess we should have brought our lunches—'cuz it looks like we're gonna be here all day!"

Chapter
7

We can't believe how people are pushing and shoving out here on Kemah Boardwalk. It's just like in New York!

"All this commotion for a gig that's not paying one red cent," grumbles an older man with several missing front teeth. He is standing on the out-of-control line directly in front of us, with his somewhat younger crony, who is a good-looking man wearing a red baseball cap and dark sunglasses.

"Don't get me wrong, though," the toothless man says. "It's not often old-timers like us get the opportunity to show our chops. Everybody wants to see you young folks." He grins shamelessly, then accidentally jabs Angie with his beat-up instrument case.

Ma winces and takes control of the situation. "Sir, maybe you should move that case off your shoulder," she says nicely.

"Oh, I'm sorry," Mr. Toothless says, apologizing sincerely, but turning and hitting Angie *again* with the case.

"Ouch," Angie says, making a comical grimace.

We look at his baseball-capped friend with pleading eyes, hoping he'll help his manner-impaired crony.

"Fred," the man says, "take Bertha off your arm and hold her in front of you, before you poke that poor girl's eye out!"

Bertha. Lord, don't tell me they are carrying body parts in that case! As if reading my mind, the man with the dark glasses says, "That's Fred's banjo—he calls her Bertha, 'cuz she's been with him for thirty-five years."

"That's right—longer than any other woman," the man called Fred says, chuckling at his own joke.

"Y'all in a group together?" Angie asks, folding her arms to protect herself from any more attacks from moving instruments.

"Yes, indeed, young lady," the younger one

says. "We're Fish 'N' Chips. He's Fred Fish. I'm Chips Carter." Mr. Carter adjusts his sunglasses and looks up at the bright, blue sky. "Young people don't listen to the kind of music we play—heart-thumpin' blues," he says.

"What instrument do *you* play?" Angie asks Mr. Chips Carter. It's hard to tell by the shape of his duffel bag—which he is smart enough to hold in *front* of him.

"I play the tambourine—shakin' up the blues."

"We always used to listen to blues music at our grandfather's house when we were little," I inform Fish 'N' Chips.

"Muddy Waters and B. B. King—Granddaddy loved them," Angie adds, grabbing on to Ma's arm.

We don't remember much about Grandaddy Selby Jasper—Ma's daddy—but we'll never forget his music. "Nothing like the blues," he used to say, playing it loud enough on the stereo so he could hear it sitting out on the porch, sipping his lemonade and watching us play in the backyard. Uncle Skeeter would bang out beats on a crate, while Angie and I hummed along, making up our own melodies.

"I guess we are the oldest fools out here," Mr. Fred Fish says to his partner.

Finally, we hear one of the security guards yelling into a bullhorn. "Listen up, people. Everybody is going to get to audition for the Montgomery Homeless Shelter Benefit. But it would help us a lot if you would just form one line against the left railing. We're getting a lot of complaints from the patrons on the Boardwalk!"

"Montgomery Homeless Shelter Benefit—is that the same thing y'all are here for?" Ma asks, concerned.

"Yes, ma'am," I tell her. "Karma's Children are performing, but all the proceeds from ticket sales are going to the Montgomery Homeless Shelter."

"Oh," Ma says, nodding her head. "I thought the benefit was for *all* the shelters in Houston."

"No, ma'am, Montgomery is the one with the most homeless women and children, so they need money to build another wing," Mr. Carter explains.

I nod my head in agreement. We know it's true, because the members of the Houston chapter of the Kats and Kittys Klub were talking about it. We still have Kats friends here—and we call them from New York every once in a while.

Now a bunch of girls are bumping into us from behind. We turn around, and almost shriek at their big gold earrings and freeze-dried curls.

"Twanda, there's no way they are gonna have all these people audition by six o'clock," one of the girls says to another, getting all upset.

What on earth are we doing out here? I wonder.

"Ma, I can't believe that you're being so nice and staying out here with us," Angie says.

"Excuse me," says one of the freeze-dried girls, poking me in the back. I never realized before that we had manner-impaired people down here too!

Ma sees the look on my face, so she addresses Miss Bo-bangles. (I'm sorry, but those are not earrings she is wearing on her ears. Those are bangles, and they belong on her arm!)

"Yes?" Ma asks politely.

"What's wrong with her? She can't talk?" one of the other girls mumbles out loud so I can hear, but I don't say a word.

The girl who poked me keeps talking. "We wuz wondering—do you think Karma's Children are going to be inside?"

"I don't know," Ma says politely, then folds her arms across the pale yellow sweater she's wearing.

"I don't know either," I say, finally speaking up for myself. I'm not afraid of these girls either.

Miss Bo-bangles sucks her teeth. "Shoot, Twanda—we shouldn't waste our time standing out here if they ain't gonna be inside. I want to get those pants down at the Galleria before they close, and I am not standing here all day."

Now another girl in the line turns, and asks someone else if Karma's Children are gonna be inside at the audition. What are they thinking? That Karma's Children would be sitting in the Crabcake Lounge, looking at all these people?

Angie looks at me and reads my thoughts. "I hope they at least stop by or something."

"With this crowd, I wouldn't count on it," Ma says sympathetically. "This is a mess."

We all take a deep breath. Now the security guards with bullhorns are walking around and *ordering* people to form "an orderly line."

"I don't think the line has moved at all," Angie moans.

"Twanda, I'm not playing—let's *go*," Miss Bo-bangle says to her friend. They are both wearing Gucci sunglasses like Ma's, but I think they are fakes.

"Not everybody is willing to work for their dreams like you girls are," Ma says when they leave. She hugs both Angie and me, which makes us feel a whole lot better for standing on a line like cattle waiting to be slaughtered.

"*We* could go get those leather pants at the Galleria, too," Angie says, imitating one of the Bo-bangle girls.

"How do you know they're *leather* pants, Angie?" I ask, chuckling.

"Well, just look at those girls, Aqua—they ain't running to the Galleria mall just to buy jogging outfits!"

Even though Ma is wearing her dark sunglasses, I can tell by the way her face is tilted that she's getting that faraway look in her eyes again. "Ma—where do you think Uncle Skeeter is?" I ask.

"I *really* wish I knew, 'cuz I'm worried sick about him—and so is Big Momma."

"After we finish with this audition, we're gonna help you find him," I promise.

I don't know what I'd do if my Daddy was as irresponsible as Uncle Skeeter. Still, Egyptian and India need their father, just as much as Angie and I need ours.

It *is* almost dark by the time we get anywhere near the front of the line. At this point, one of the attendants hands us a form to fill out.

"Come on, Fish 'N' Chips—you know it's your turn to sing for us," Ma chides the blues singers. Truth is, they've been entertaining us on and off for the past few hours—which otherwise would have seemed like *years*.

Almost everybody on line has been doing some singing, but I don't mind telling you *our* performance got a bit of a standing ovation. Even so, Fish 'N' Chips got the most applause by far. I think most of the young people in the line had never heard anything like their music!

"All right, Fred—let's give the young ladies—and that includes you, too—a taste of the blues," Mr. Chips says, winking at Ma.

Omigod—I think he likes her! "See, Ma, I told you those statistics were incorrect," I tease her.

"Well, what do you expect? He can't half see behind those shades," Ma jokes. "Okay, then, let's hear it," she says, turning back to Fish 'N' Chips.

"Duh-do, duh-do," Fred starts warming up, then Chips joins in, and Fish 'N' Chips start frying up another blues song:

"I went down to the store to get a root beer
But when I came back, nobody was near
Not my woman, not my banjo, and not my dear
Then one of my neighbors made it real clear
He said, son, you done lost your woman
   to a bad case of the blues
The next time you go to the store
   you'd better look at the news
I said, I lost my woman to a bad case of the blues
And maybe that's why she ran off with my shoes
I've got those lost-woman blues
   those dirty, lowdown, lost-woman blues!"

We clap up a storm, because Fish 'N' Chips deserve it! They sure seem to make Ma happy, too. She almost seems like her old self again. "Why don't y'all come on over Tuesday night for some pre-Thanksgiving dinner?" Ma asks them both.

"Well, I reckon we could," Mr. Chips says, winking at Ma again. "What do you think, Fred, have we lost our heads?"

Fred chuckles loudly at his partner's joke.

"Well, Miss . . . uh . . ." Mr. Chips pauses, because he doesn't know what to call Ma. He probably thinks she's married.

"Call me Junifred," Ma says, her eyes twinkling.

I gasp. I haven't heard Ma call herself that in *years*!

"Well, Junifred, we would be delighted to accept that invitation!" Mr. Chips says, beside himself.

"What part of our town do y'all live in?" Ma asks them.

Fish 'N' Chips just sorta pause and look at each other. "Well, we live over by Montgomery," Mr. Chips says quietly.

"Oh, y'all live over by the shelter?" Ma asks.

"No, ma'am," Mr. Fish says, taking over for his partner, who has become speechless. "We live at the shelter."

I'm so embarrassed. We didn't know they were homeless!

"Well, that's fine," Ma says, not backing

down from her invitation. "If you need a ride to my house Tuesday night, just let me know. Otherwise, I expect to see the two of you at my dinner table around eight o'clock!"

We are so proud of Ma. Now I wish the rest of the Cheetah Girls could meet *our* mother— they would be proud of her too!

"Gentlemen, could you step inside?" says a security attendant to Fish 'N' Chips.

"Well, ladies, it looks like it's curtain time," Mr. Fred Fish says, as the two of them go inside for their audition.

We wish them good luck—and we really mean it. Fish 'N' Chips sure earned their tartar sauce tonight! I start humming a bar from their song as we wait for our turn.

After about fifteen minutes, Fish 'N' Chips re-emerge in the doorway of the Crabcake Lounge. Ma seems genuinely happy to see them again. "Why don't you two wait out here with me, while the girls go inside?" she suggests to them.

Angie and I grin from ear to ear as we are ushered into the Crabcake Lounge for our audition. "I'll be waiting right here!" Ma yells after us.

The first thing I notice when we get inside is the stacks of forms. They are piled in big bins on top of a table with a checkered paper tablecloth. The place really looks a plain mess.

I can feel the disappointment in my heart when I look around and don't see Karma's Children. I knew they weren't here, because we would've seen them come in. But somehow, I guess I held out hope that they were hiding under the bar or something.

Angie and I smooth down our cheetah skirts, and stand quietly on the tiny stage until we're addressed. There are about six people sitting at the tables talking, and a few more running around, busy doing things.

"Okay," says one of the ladies, who is wearing a ten-gallon cowboy hat, a fringed jacket, and a badge that says VOLUNTEER.

"You girls are . . . ?" the lady asks, then pauses, obviously waiting for us to fill in the blank.

"Angi—" my slow sister starts in.

"The Cheetah Girls," I say, thinking quickly. That's what the lady wants to hear—the name of our group. "My sister was trying to say that she's Anginette and I'm Aquanette Walker— but we're the Cheetah Girls. The other members of our group are in New York—you know, for the holidays."

"Ah, yes," the cowboy hat lady says. "You girls are from Houston though, right?"

"Yes, ma'am, we are," I say proudly.

"Good—because 'Houston Helps Its Own' is the name of the benefit concert, as you may have heard by now," the lady continues.

"Yes, ma'am, we know." I nod again.

A man with thick glasses and a bright red tie clears his throat. He seems to be getting impatient. They are probably tired and irritated after seeing hundreds of people all day.

"Well, would you mind singing for us now?" the lady asks.

"You mean, just a capella?" I ask.

"Yes, that would be fine."

"Oh." I nod, then move toward Angie so we can begin our two-part harmony. Why didn't we rehearse a gospel song? I wonder, shrieking inside. Maybe our kinda of music isn't appropriate for a homeless benefit! No, that's ridiculous, I assure myself.

Angie is looking at me, waiting to begin. So are all the auditioners. We sing "It's Raining Benjamins," and by the time we get to the second verse, they all seem to be smiling. Some of them are even keeping time with their hands and feet. That gives us confidence, and we really lay into the chorus:

"*It's raining Benjamins*
For a change and some coins
It's raining Benjamins
I heard that, so let's join
It's raining Benjamins . . . again!"

The volunteer lady starts clapping, then the others join in. "Wonderful, girls. We'll let you know," she says enthusiastically. "We've got to move along now, but it was great meeting you."

"How many groups are they gonna pick?" I ask as we're leaving.

"Well, we want to give as many groups a chance as we can," the nice volunteer lady rambles on.

"Each group will get to do one song," the man in the glasses and red tie explains, getting more to the point. "We plan on having about three to five warm-up spots."

"Oh, well, thank you," I gush, even though

I'm not exactly sure what he means. Then, remembering my manners, I ask the lady her name, so I can say good night to her properly.

"Oh, I'm sorry—I'm Mrs. Fenilworth, and this is Mr. Paddlewheel."

"Good night, Mrs. Fenilworth. Good night, Mr. Paddlewheel."

Once we're outside, Angie asks, "When he said warm-up spots, that's what we were auditioning for, right?"

"I guess so. Thank goodness, we've got spots to spare!"

We see Ma standing by the railing with Fish 'N' Chips, a little way from the crowd. We are so happy to see them that we hug all three of them one after another.

Ma wants to know all about the audition, but Angie and I have only one thing on our minds right now. "Let's go eat!" we scream at Ma in unison. We're always hungry after we perform—just like real cheetahs!

Chapter 8

Big Momma calls first thing in the morning, and this time we can really hear the strain in her voice. "I'm praying for Skeeter," she says, sobbing. I can just see her wringing her good handkerchief in her hands—the one she keeps balled up in her skirt pocket and takes out for "sneezing and wheezing."

"Big Momma, don't you have any idea where he could be?" I ask, getting so anxious I can hardly contain myself.

"I've called everybody that knows that boy, and nobody has seen hide nor hair of him," Big Momma says sadly.

"What about, um, a lady friend?" I ask gingerly.

"You know he never brought her around

here—which means she ain't no Christian woman," Big Momma says gruffly.

"We're praying for him, Big Momma," I say, sniffling into the phone. "We love you."

Ma comes over to me, sits down at the table, and puts down her coffee mug. She takes the phone from my hand. "No news?" she asks, then listens. "Hang on, Momma—that's my other line beeping. Someone's trying to get through. Yes, I *have* to get it. Just hold on for a minute."

That makes Angie smile. Big Momma hates call waiting. "If the line is busy, let 'em call back!" she always insists. She refuses to get call waiting on her phone, and sometimes it takes us hours to reach her!

"This is Mrs. Walk— um, Junifred speaking," Ma says to someone on the other line. She still seems confused about what to call herself, now that she and Daddy are dee-vorced. "Could you hang on a second please?" Ma says to the person on the phone, then clicks to the other line, "Momma, a lady is calling for the girls on the other line. Hmm. Hmm. Call me as soon as you hear something. Hmm. Hmm. What? Yes, I'll tell them."

Ma clicks the line and hands us the phone, chuckling. "Big Momma says Porgy and Bess have worn out their welcome. She said it'll take her two years to replant the strawberry patch they trampled to death!"

"Yes, ma'am," I say quickly, hardly even paying attention. I grab the receiver from her and greet the person on the line. "Hello?"

"Yes, this is Mrs. Fenilworth, from the 'Houston Helps Its Own' Committee?'"

"Hi, Mrs. Fenilworth! This is Aquanette Walker," I say, suddenly getting a jittery feeling in my stomach.

"Well, Miss Walker—we had a really hard time narrowing down all the candidates for the benefit concert," Mrs. Fenilworth says, very slowly.

Oh, no—we didn't get it! I let out a big sigh. Oh, well, at least she was nice enough to call and let us know.

"There were just so many wonderful performers from our fine city," Mrs. Fenilworth rambles on, "but we had to think about what would be, um, the best complement for Karma's Children—and that's how we finally decided on picking you girls."

The Cheetah Girls

Did she say what I thought she said? "Do you mean you picked us out of all those people?" I ask, holding my breath.

"Well, we have narrowed it down to five groups, but yes, we thought your group—the, um, Cheetah Girls—would be a nice addition. That is, if you're still interested. We understand that there is no money involved, so it could be difficult—"

I just start screaming my head off.

"Miss Walker?"

"I'm so sorry, Mrs. Fenilworth, but you have no idea what this means to the Cheetah Girls!" Then I suddenly realize—what about the rest of the Cheetah Girls? We can't perform onstage without the others—that just wouldn't be right!

Angie grabs the receiver from me. "Hi, Mrs. Fenilworth, this is Anginette Walker—did you say *all* the Cheetah Girls could come? No, they live in New York—but if you paid for their plane tickets, they'd be here tomorrow!"

I look at Angie in disbelief. Has she lost her mind? I turn to Ma, who is just sitting there, smiling and shaking her head.

"No, no. We have plenty of room for them to stay at our house. Hmm. Hmm. Okay. Bye."

"Mrs. Fenilworth is gonna let us know if they'll pay to fly the Cheetah Girls from New York to Houston!" Angie screams.

"That's real good, Angie," Ma says, delighted. "And good for you for having the courage to ask!"

"Angie, what if they change their minds about using us because of what you just did?" I ask my sister, stunned.

"If Fish 'N' Chips can stick together for thirty-five years, then so can the Cheetah Girls—all *five* of us!" Angie insists proudly.

The phone rings, and all three of us jump up. Ma is first to grab it. "Hello?" she says. "Yes, this is their mother. Oh, that's wonderful news! The girls will be so pleased! Uh-huh. Let me get a pen. Well, the girls do have a manager—I'll tell her to call you and make the travel arrangements. Uh-huh . . ." Ma continues writing furiously on a notepad.

I motion to her to give me the phone. "That's real good news, Mrs. Fenilworth!" I exclaim.

"Well, it's the least we could do, since you girls are giving your time and talent for such a good cause," Mrs. Fenilworth says.

"Um, Mrs. Fenilworth, what are some of the

other groups you've picked?"

"Let me get the list," Mrs. Fenilworth says. I can hear her shuffling some papers, then she returns. "We have 'Diamonds in the Ruff'— they are so cute—older girls than you, I think. Um, Miggy and Mo', Moody Gardens, and— oh, that's it. Funny, I thought there were five. . . ."

"Well, Mrs. Fenilworth," I say, sounding professional, "while we were waiting to audition, we had the pleasure of hearing this amazing blues group, Fish 'N' Chips."

"Uh, yes, I remember them," Mrs. Fenilworth says, hesitating. "We thought they were very good, but perhaps . . . not appropriate as an opening act for, um, the Karma's Children audience."

"Well, Mrs. Fenilworth, we are only thirteen, and we *love* them. My generation isn't just interested in R & B, rap, and pop music—we love the blues, too!" I try not to look at Angie, who is making me laugh, hopping around with her hand over her mouth.

"Of course," Mrs. Fenilworth says, like she's trying not to say anything to offend me. She *is* nice.

"And you know Houston does help its

own—everyone is real proud of Fish 'N' Chips at the Montgomery Homeless Shelter—where they *live*, tirelessly helping the other residents and cheering them up with their music."

"They *live* at Montgomery?" Mrs. Fenilworth asks, surprised. "They never mentioned that."

"Well, they are proud, fine musicians first of all—so I'm not surprised they didn't say anything about living in a homeless shelter."

"Let me see what I can do—because your point is very well taken, young lady. If I can pull a few strings here, we'll contact the gentlemen ourselves, okay?" Mrs. Fenilworth says. "Um . . . do you have any *more* requests?"

"Oh, no, ma'am!" I reply quickly. "We, um, the Cheetah Girls look forward to seeing you at the rehearsal, Mrs. Fenilworth—and we can't thank you enough!"

"*OMIGOD!!*" Angie and I hug each other like two cuddly teddy bears.

"That was real nice what you did, Nettie One," Ma says to me—and now I'm beaming, because I've made her proud, too.

The phone rings *again*. "Well, pick it up. Don't look at me—I just live here," Ma says, half smiling. I think she's afraid to pick it up, to tell you the truth—'cuz it might be bad news about Uncle Skeeter.

"Hello?" I say apprehensively.

"Anginette?"

"No, it's Aquanette," I say to Big Momma, who sounds upset.

"Put Junie on the phone," she says quietly.

Ma sees the fear on my face as I pass her the phone. "What is it?" she asks, while we look on. "On Sycamore Road? Yeah, that's all we can do now, sit and wait."

Ma hangs up, and we can feel her heaviness. All the excitement about performing at Karma's Children Benefit Concert has flown out of the room like fairy dust.

"We've got to go on with our lives until we know more, Aquanette," Ma explains, calling me by my full name, which she only does when she's being real serious. "You'd better call Galleria and get this rodeo in motion." She hands me the phone to call New York.

"Yes, ma'am," I say, trying to shake the bad case of the spookies that has come over me.

"Houston is boostin,' baby!" Galleria exclaims excitedly when I tell her the good news. "Now I know that dreams do come true in the jiggy jungle, because I've been *praying* for a way to get out of Dodge for Thanksgiving!"

I try to calm my nerves down as I tell Galleria all about Fish 'N' Chips, Mrs. Fenilworth, Mr. Paddlewheel . . .

All of a sudden, Galleria interrupts, blurting out, "Miz Aquanette, what's wrong? You don't really sound like yourself. If you don't want us to come and perform with you . . . we'll understand."

I am shocked that Galleria thinks we don't want the rest of the Cheetah Girls to come down and perform with us. "Oh, no! It's not that," I reassure her. "But there is something wrong. Our uncle Skeeter hasn't come home for five days. He hasn't even called his kids—our cousins Egyptian and India. Now we found out that his car has been spotted on Sycamore Road, but we don't know anybody who lives over there."

"Don't you worry, Aqua," Galleria says confidently. "When we get there, and once we take care of our business, we're gonna put our Cheetah Girl heads together and get to the bottom of this."

Angie talks to Galleria for a few minutes, and

then we *finally* sit down to eat breakfast. I feel so overwhelmed by everything that is happening that I don't know if I should cry or laugh. I know we're only singing one song in the benefit, but it's a *big* deal. And I know Uncle Skeeter is probably okay, but that is a big deal too. Please God, help us through this.

Ma gets up from the table and puts the phone in the living room. "I don't want to hear another phone ring all day!" she says.

"Amen to that!" Angie and I say together.

Chapter 9

We're disappointed Ms. Dorothea can't come down with Galleria, Chanel, and Dorinda to Houston. Galleria, on the other hand, is tickled silly to be away from her mother.

"Free at last!" she screams, practically jumping on top of me when we meet her at the airport.

"Have you seen Karma's Children yet?" Chanel asks.

"No, we haven't," I assure her. "You'll be the first to know when they hit Kemah Boardwalk—you and everybody else!"

"Girls, I hope you don't mind, but we're

gonna have to take you right over to rehearsal first," Ma informs our friends.

"That's cool-io with us," Dorinda says.

Ma chuckles, "You girls have such a cute way of talking!"

"That's how we flow in the Big Apple!" Galleria shouts.

"*Gracias pooches*, for letting us come stay with you," Chanel says, making Ma chuckle some more.

"You're quite welcome. I haven't seen my girls this excited before—about *anything*!"

Angie and I start talking a mile a minute about everything that has happened so far. Dorinda is especially keen on hearing about Fish 'N' Chips.

"You actually got them on the bill with us?" she asks, surprised.

"Well, hopefully we did!" I say. "You should have seen the committee's faces when we sang 'It's Raining Benjamins.' At first, we thought we picked the wrong song—"

"Hold up," says a breathless Galleria. "You told them we're gonna sing 'It's Raining Benjamins?'"

"Why, yes," I say, flustered.

"Aqua, you can't make those kind of decisions without us!" Galleria says, getting agitated. "*I'm* the one—I mean, *we* decide *together* what numbers we're going to perform."

Everybody gets real quiet. Now I know exactly how Chanel feels when Galleria rags on her!

"Well, what's done is done," Galleria huffs, giving up for once. Thank gooseness.

"Ooh, look at all the water!" Dorinda coos as we pull up to Kemah's Boardwalk.

"This is Galveston Bay," Angie says proudly. "You should see it in the spring when all the flowers are in full bloom—it almost looks like a tropical paradise."

"Word. I *feel* like I'm in paradise," Dorinda chuckles.

"Y'all are staying for the rest of the holiday weekend, aren't you?" Ma asks, like she's not taking no for an answer.

"Yeah!!!" Galleria, Chanel, and Dorinda say in unison. Angie and I smile at each other. Who woulda thought *we* would be showing *them* the time of their lives?

"Here we are," Angie says, as we pull into the parking lot of the Crabcake Lounge.

"This is so dope," Dorinda says, marveling at everything. Walking through the parking lot, we pass a group of people wearing cowboy hats, fringed jackets, and boots. "Word, look at their outfits!"

"You know the rodeo is real big in Houston," I explain to the New York Cheetah Girls. "Everybody has at least one cowboy hat and pair of boots."

"Well, howdy doody, I'm diggin' it," Galleria says, tipping an imaginary hat to the ten-gallon cowboy hoofers, who are staring at us like we're the main attraction in the rodeo!

"Everybody is feeling our cheetah-ness!" I exclaim.

"There they are!" Angie says, spotting Fish 'N' Chips. "Look, they're playing!"

Fish 'N' Chips are holding court for the tourists walking by. Mr. Fred Fish is plucking on his banjo and Mr. Chips Carter is shaking his tambourine. Mr. Fred's banjo case is opened and lying on the ground. A few tourists throw change into it.

As soon as Fish 'N' Chips see us, they light up as bright as a Christmas tree. Then they circle around us, and start singing up a storm:

*"I went down to the store to get a root beer
But when I came back, nobody was near
Not my woman, not my banjo, and not my dear
Then one of my neighbors made it real clear
He said, son, you done lost your woman
    to a bad case of the blues
The next time you go to the store
    you'd better look at the news
I said, I lost my woman to a bad case of the blues
And maybe that's why she ran off with my shoes
I've got those lost-woman blues
    those dirty, lowdown, lost-woman blues!"*

Galleria, Chanel, and Dorinda are grinning from ear to ear and clapping.

"See?" I tell Angie, "I *told* Mrs. Fenilworth we young people can groove to the blues—it's just in our blood!"

"Can you believe they picked a couple of old-timers like us, out of all them younguns?" Mr. Fish exclaims.

Angie and I grin like two foxes who've swallowed some hens. I poke her, just to make sure she doesn't say a word to Fish 'N' Chips about us pulling a few strings. I'm just grateful we had a few strings to pull!

I look at Dorinda, and see tears welling in her eyes. "Can I see that?" she asks, pointing to Mr. Fred's banjo.

"Sure thing, little lady."

Dorinda is just fascinated with Mr. Fish's instrument. We all sit on the railing and watch, while he shows her how to play.

"Now, when you pluck the banjo to play the blues, you gotta *feel* the blues—you know, slump down some, and think about all the people who done you wrong," Mr. Fish says, grinning his toothless grin.

"Word. That won't be too hard," Dorinda says, slumping her tiny little shoulders and putting a funny scowl on her face.

"Now just make up any words you want, so you can get the melody to match the plucking."

"Um, okay—um, let's see:

"I'm sitting on the porch
just minding my bizness
trying to light a torch
For my big ole' horse
But my dern little cat
keeps coming back.
I can't get no slack

for my wack attack blues!!
I said, I can't get no slack
for m-y-y-y wack-attack blluuues!"

A tourist stops to listen, and puts another dollar in Fish 'N' Chips' banjo case! We all start howling at Dorinda.

"Well now, that's interesting how you got the rap mixing up with the blues," Mr. Fred Fish says, tickled.

We are laughing so hard that we don't see Mrs. Fenilworth motioning for us to come in for rehearsal. Ma taps us on the shoulder and points to where Mrs. Fenilworth is standing quietly, waiting for us to finish.

Mr. Fred Fish seems a little embarrassed by the money in his banjo case, and he shovels it quickly into a pouch he takes out of his pocket.

Suddenly a light goes off in my head—this is probably how they make money to live—by singing on the streets!

Two little girls with pigtails and freckles come inside behind us, and sit down at one of the tables. "Hi, we're Miggy and Mo'!" the more freckly one says. I wonder if they're fraternal twins. They must be sisters, and they look really young.

"Hi, we're the Cheetah Girls," Chanel says, real friendly.

"Mr. Paddlewheel, is everybody here?" Mrs. Fenilworth asks.

"No—we're missing the Moody Gardens."

All of a sudden, three boys wearing plaid shirts and jeans barge into the Crabcake Lounge. "Uh, sorry we're late."

"Just take a seat," Mr. Paddlewheel says nicely. "Tomorrow night," he tells us all, "we are throwing a very special benefit concert, to help raise money for Houston's homeless population. The benefit, we are happy to report, is *completely* sold out, and we are expecting an estimated five thousand people to fill the Turtle Dome Arena out in back. You have been selected to sing one song each—sort of a tribute to Houston's burgeoning undiscovered talent, and the possibilities that lie ahead of all of us."

Five thousand people! I swallow hard just thinking about it. We've never performed for that many folks at once!

"What's the game plan now?" Galleria asks

excitedly, as we head back to Ma's car.

"Well, I'm making some crawfish and pota-toes stew for dinner, if anyone is interested," Ma chuckles.

"Yes, bring on Mr. Crawdaddy!" Galleria shouts.

"Gentlemen, that invitation still holds." Ma is talking to Fish 'N' Chips, who are about to walk out of the parking lot. I'll bet you they walk all the way back to Montgomery Shelter, since they don't have a car!

"We'll be there, Ms. Junifred, don't you worry," Mr. Chips Carter says. Lifting his sun-glasses, he gives her a wink. "Yes, indeed. Wouldn't miss it for the world."

"Wow, this is *la dopa!*" Chanel exclaims, "It looks like right out of a magazine."

I guess we forget how pretty Ma's house is. It's so country and flowery—the exact opposite of Daddy's apartment in New York.

"Don't mind the mess," Ma says, moving some mail off the table. As she does, she looks at one of the envelopes. "I've got to mail this census form in," she says, putting it aside.

"The ones who don't get counted are usually

the really poor people," Angie explains to Dorinda.

"So what?" Dorinda asks.

"Well, see, how much money the government gives Houston depends on how many people say they live here. So when poor people don't fill out their census forms, the government gives less money to help the poor."

"Oh," Dorinda says, and you can tell it makes her feel sad.

We sit down in the living room while Ma starts getting ready to cook dinner. Fish 'N' Chips will be coming over later, and she wants everything to be perfect, so there's a lot for her to do.

Meanwhile, Galleria wants to hear about the whole Skeeter business. I tell her about his red Cadillac being spotted on Sycamore Road.

Ma hears us talking about him, and she reminds us of his last words to her: "He said he was tired of everything, and just wanted to 'rest in peace.' That's why we are so frightened at what he might do."

"Don't forget what India said, about Uncle Skeeter's girlfriend having a name that's softer than mink," Angie adds, trying to be helpful. "And what Big Momma said about her last name being Wilkerson."

"Don't snooze on the clues!" Galleria exclaims, and we can see the lightbulb going off in her head. "Get me a phone book—you'd be surprised by who has a listed number."

Angie and I just look at Galleria like, "What on earth are you talking about?"

"Your mother says her last name is Wilkerson, right?"

"Yeah . . . so?"

"So, let's see if she's in the phone book."

"Galleria, do you know how many Wilkersons there are in the Houston phone book? That's a *typical* Southern last name!" I'm starting to get exasperated by Galleria's over-eagerness. Of course, I should have known she would have a plan.

"Yeah, but how many of those Wilkersons have a first name that's softer than mink?"

Now we all look at Galleria in awe. Why didn't *we* think of that?

"Let's look at every Wilkerson in the phone book!" Chanel says excitedly.

We huddle around, going down the names of Wilkersons carefully and reading them out loud—"Annabel, Karen, Katie, Sandy, Sable, Twanda, Toinette—"

"Wait a minute," Dorinda says. "Go back—*Sable!* Remember what India said? 'Soft as mink.' Well, sable is a kind of fur, and so is mink."

"Omigod," gasps Angie. "Look. She lives on Hummingbird—that's right around the corner from Sycamore!"

"We've gotta think of a plan," Ma muses.

"I've got an idea," Galleria says with a satisfied smirk. "We go over there, and say we're from the Census Bureau, and that we need her to fill out a form, because people aren't handing them in on time. Your Mom could be the census lady—and we'll be her kids. She can say she's working late to earn extra money or something."

"Oh, I get it—get her sympathy and wheedle our way in. Then, when Ma wins her confidence, they can do girl talk—about their boyfriends, right?" It sounds like a good plan to me.

"Yeah!" Galleria says.

"But what if she recognizes Ma?" Angie asks, concerned, even though Ma has obviously never met Sable.

"She's not going to recognize your mother," Chanel says.

"Why?" we ask in unison.

"Because we're gonna put her in a Cheetah Girl disguise, just in case, *mamacitas*!"

"I haven't had so much fun playing dress-up since I was a kid," Ma says while we fuss with her. We wrap her hair in a cheetah turban and try on a pair of cheetah sunglasses.

"Well," Ma says, looking in the mirror. "It sure doesn't look like me—I guess it's worth a shot. But I don't have too long—I've got to get dinner together, remember."

"Don't forget the form," Dorinda says, handing Ma the envelope with the census form inside.

"Oh, right—and I should take my clipboard from work, and my briefcase," she adds.

I can tell Ma is feeling much better—at least we're *doing* something about finding Uncle Skeeter, instead of sitting around thinking the worst.

"I think it's best if Dorinda and I pretend to be your ma's daughters," Galleria says. "Just in case Skeeter already told Sable that he has twin nieces."

Even though I feel disappointed, I know Bubbles is right about that. Uncle Skeeter does love bragging about us to everybody, just like Big Momma.

"Why can't *I* be one of the daughters?" Chanel asks, feeling left out, too.

"'Cuz, Chuchie, you have a Spanish accent—maybe Sable won't buy that you're Ms. Walker's daughter."

"Oh—I've got to change my name," Ma says. "I'll say my name is Mrs. Cobbler—that way I won't forget, 'cuz I was planning on making y'all a cobbler for Thanksgiving Day." Ma seems amused by her own cleverness.

"Okay, 'Mom,' let's go," Galleria says, taking Ma by the arm. Suddenly I feel jealous—but then I catch myself for being so selfish.

When we drive past Sycamore Road, we see that Uncle Skeeter's car is still parked there. I get a bad case of the spookies again, and take a deep breath. Ma keeps driving until we get to Hummingbird Road, and Sable Wilkerson's house. There, she pulls over and cuts the engine.

"Someone's home," Angie says quietly.

"Good luck," I whisper as Ma, Galleria, and Dorinda get out the car.

There are kids playing on the sidewalk, and they check out the three of them as they walk up to Sable's front porch.

Angie, Chanel, and I sit in the car on lookout. The plan is that if we see Uncle Skeeter going into the house, or sneaking out the back, we honk the horn.

It seems like hours before Ma, Galleria, and Dorinda come out. I can tell by the way they're walking that they've had no luck with their census charade.

"She's more clueless than we are," Ma says, visibly upset as she gets into the driver's seat. "She hasn't seen Skeeter in five days." Ma's hands are shaking as she tries to put the keys in the ignition. She stops, then puts her head down on the steering wheel, and starts bawling like a baby.

Galleria puts her arms around Ma's shoulders, and we just sit and wait until she pulls herself together. I bite my lower lip. I don't want to start crying too.

"What are we going to do?" Angie says, feeling as helpless as I do.

"Exactly what we were doing before—wait," Ma says, pulling herself together and taking a deep breath. She's all right for the moment, ready to concentrate on driving home.

The sadness looms over all of us. All of sudden, it doesn't matter that we are going to sing a song in front of five thousand people tomorrow night. All that matters is that we find Uncle Skeeter—and that he's all right.

Chapter
10

The next morning, the gloomy cloud is still hanging over our heads even though we had a great dinner the night before with Fish 'N' Chips. They ate everything but the tablecloth! We got ready to go see Granddaddy Walker at his funeral parlor. (He's seventy-two years old, and has never missed a day of work!) Granddaddy Walker has been chomping at the bit, because we have been four whole days in Houston and still haven't come to see him.

"Let's go wake up the dead!" Galleria says, when we tell her about his hurt feelings.

Dorinda is excited about going, too. "We might as well take a 'coffin break' before the show," she smirks.

"Now remember girls, we can't stay too long," Ma preps us.

I don't know why she says that, because we have plenty of time. We have ironed our costumes, bought the cheetah umbrellas we're gonna hold, and the play money we're going to throw onstage for our performance, and we've practiced "It's Raining Benjamins" till we could sing it backward.

But I guess Ma feels bad about the dee-vorce and all, even though Granddaddy Walker still treats her like family, and we know he loves us, well, "to death."

Rest in Peace is the biggest funeral parlor in Houston, and it's housed in the landmark district, in a beautiful building with a white marble front, and white pillars on the porch. When we get inside, Granddaddy Walker gives Ma a real long hug and doesn't let go.

"We'll get through this, Junifred. We sure will," he tells her. Obviously, Ma has already told him about Uncle Skeeter.

"Should we call the police?" Ma asks him, distraught.

"No—not yet. The Lord will tell you what to do—just wait and see," Granddaddy Walker says, laying down words of wisdom like he always does.

"Good morning," says Grandma Selma, greeting us all cheerfully. She is Granddaddy Walker's second wife, and also his secretary. He married her after Grandma Winnie passed (which raised a few eyebrows—since Selma is twenty-four years younger than he is!).

Granddaddy Walker peers over his bifocals to look at me and my friends. "How y'all doing?" he says, grinning and extending his hand to shake Galleria's.

Bubbles seems a little nervous, acting very polite and looking down at the floor. I guess Granddaddy Walker can seem a little intimidating. He is a great big man, and he always wears a black suit with a white shirt, and a red handkerchief in the jacket pocket. You can tell how important he is just by the way he looks.

"You know, that boy hasn't been himself since his daddy died," Granddaddy says, shaking his head.

All of a sudden, Galleria is looking straight at Granddaddy Walker, and watching him real closely. "Skeeter's father died?" she asks, her eyes narrowing.

"Oh, yes, seven years ago. I buried him myself. Skeeter loved his daddy something awful," Granddaddy goes on.

Galleria looks at the literature laying on the table, then mutters, "'Rest in Peace . . .' that's what Skeeter said . . . ."

"What?" I ask Galleria, confused.

"Your ma said Skeeter was acting strange the last time she saw him, and he told her, 'I'm tired. I just want to rest in peace.'"

"Yeah," Ma says, wondering what Galleria is getting at.

"So Skeeter's father had a funeral service here at Rest in Peace Funeral Home," Galleria continues, talking out loud. "Where did you bury him?"

"Where I bury everybody—at the Creekmore Cemetery, about ten miles from here," Granddaddy Walker says, his big voice booming. "Of course, Selby Jasper's coffin is buried in his own mausoleum—the biggest one in the cemetery."

"I think we should go over there and take a look," Galleria says, like she's onto something.

"Go to the cemetery? Now?" Angie asks, surprised.

"I think we'd better," I say, sticking up for Galleria. I know she's like a dog with a bone. When Miss Galleria is onto something, she won't leave it alone. Let her sniff around Granddaddy Selby's grave—maybe she will come up with something.

"At this point, I'm willing to try anything that will help us find my brother," Ma blurts out. "The worst that could happen is I get to visit my Daddy's grave, and y'all get to do some sightseeing at a cemetery!"

"Take a bunch of magnolias with you," Grandma Selma says, pointing to some beautiful purple flowers in a vase on the table.

Granddaddy Walker picks up the phone and calls Willie, who drives the hearses for all the funeral processions to the cemetery. "Willie, we're gonna need a hearse—bring out the best one we have."

Then he puts his arms around Angie and me. "Willie will drive y'all to Creekmore," he says, his eyes twinkling. He knows how much Angie and I love riding in his big, black hearses, with their cushioned seats and draped windows.

"You sure about that, Granddaddy Walker?" Ma asks. Now that she and Daddy are dee-vorced,

I don't think she likes asking Granddaddy Walker for anything.

"Yes, Junifred, I'm sure," Granddaddy Walker says, his eyes twinkling. "No 'body' is in a hurry this week."

After burying half the dead people in Houston, Granddaddy Walker has quite a sense of humor about corpses. That's just one more reason why we love him. Angie smiles, then looks down, trying to be respectful.

"Wow, this is supa dupa cushy," Dorinda says as we climb into the hearse.

"This is the biggest one I've been in!" Chanel coos.

"Chuchie, you've *never* been in one," Galleria says, shaking her head.

"I know," Chanel responds, grinning sheepishly. "That's what I meant."

"Just sit back and relax, girls. Willie's gonna take good care of ya," the driver says, looking at us in the rearview mirror. Willie looks spiffy in his black uniform with matching black chauffeur's hat and white gloves. We tell him all about our singing group, as he takes the long, scenic route to Creekmore Cemetery.

"I used to play the keyboards when I was younger—with a group of my boys," Willie chuckles. "Nothing serious like you Cheetah Girls are doing. 'Cheetah Girls'—that sounds catchy, all right."

"Catch the rising stars while you can!" Galleria giggles.

"You know, Skeeter used to play the keyboards when we were kids," Ma says. "He was always beating or strumming on something. But Daddy was always telling him to get a serious job—be somebody. So Skeeter gave it up, and went to work for the sanitation department."

"I remember Uncle Skeeter always pounding out beats on cans and things," I say, "when Granddaddy was playing his blues music. Uncle Skeeter liked the blues a whole lot."

"Oh, yeah—that's his favorite music," Ma says, getting tearful again.

"You girls should keep singing—keep following your dreams, even when it seems people are trying to take them from you," Willie the driver says, like he knows what he's talking about.

I look at Chanel, who is sitting next to me,

and smile at her. I wonder if Willie's dreams have come true. I sure don't think Uncle Skeeter's dreams have . . .

Tears well in my eyes. I stare out of the window as we drive past the big wrought-iron gates into the cemetery.

Chanel grabs my hand tighter. "Look at all the tombstones—all those people who can't have fun anymore, like we do," she says wistfully.

"The most famous people in Houston are buried here. Yes, indeed," Willie says, driving real slow so he can show us some of the tombstones as we pass. "That mausoleum right there the permanent home of the Great Abra Cadabra—one of the greatest magicians that ever lived. And there's where General Sam Houston rests. This city is named after him. And here . . . is your mausoleum." He pulls over and we get out of the hearse.

"It's so quiet here," Dorinda says, taking in the peaceful scene.

"If you listen real quietly, you can hear the souls whispering," Willie chuckles, then starts humming a gospel hymn. We all walk down the lane where Granddaddy Selby Jasper's mausoleum stands. "I'll be waiting right here for you," Willie says softly. "Take your time."

Ma sets the bunch of magnolias down in front of the mausoleum. As we walk up to the entrance, we see that the door is slightly ajar!

"I can't believe this," Ma says, freezing in her tracks. "One thing is for sure, *someone* has been here."

"Should we go inside?" I ask, quivering. Angie is holding my hand. Chanel has grabbed Galleria's, and poor Dorinda is just standing in the background, like she's ready to run if she has to. We look around, but there isn't one person in sight except us and Willie.

"I think we're out here all by ourselves," Angie says. Taking a big gulp, she folds her arms across her chest, like she's bracing herself for whatever comes popping out from behind a tombstone.

"Well, let's get to it," Ma says, pulling on the heavy mausoleum door.

The door creaks all the way open, and a few cobwebs fall on Ma's head. We peer inside behind her, but we can't really see anything, it's so dark. "Can *you* see anything, Ma?" I ask, shuddering.

"No, but—aaaah!" Ma screams, then takes a step back. "I heard something—I think it's a mouse!" We are all deathly afraid of mice, more than of any ghoul or goblin, that's for sure.

"I think we need a flashlight to go inside," Ma says, backing out.

We hear a rustling sound again. There's definitely something crawling around in there! "Hello!" Ma yells deep into the mausoleum. "Is anybody in there?"

We hear more stirring. "Ms. Walker, I don't think that's a mouse, 'cuz it moves every time you say something!" Galleria says, squinting her eyes and trying to get a peek.

"I think you're right—and I have a feeling I know exactly *who* it is," Ma says sharply. I can tell she isn't afraid anymore. "Skeeter—I know you're in there, so you can stop hiding!"

We wait for what seems like years, and then we hear a noise again—this time it sounds like a bottle rolling on the ground inside.

"Skeeter, I'm not playing. Whatever is wrong, we can work this out," Ma says, determined not to back down.

"All right . . ." we hear a man's voice grumble. "Shoot, it figures *you* would find me!"

Ma gasps, and puts her hand over her mouth. Tears well up in her eyes. "Skeeter—Omigod, I can't believe this!"

"Yeah, I can't believe it either. I'll be right out."

We back away from inside Granddaddy Selby's mausoleum and wait. And wait . . .

"Maybe he's not gonna come out,' Angie whispers.

But a moment later, like a ghost from Thanksgiving past, Uncle Skeeter emerges from the mausoleum. Believe me, he *looks* like a ghost!

We try not to let the shock show in our eyes, but we can't help it. Uncle Skeeter's eyes are bloodshot, his face is full of whiskers, and his clothes are all wrinkled. He scratches his head, like he has lice or something, and asks sheepishly, "Who are all these people?"

"These are Nettie One and Two's friends from New York," Ma says defensively, then she bursts into tears. "Why didn't you come talk to me, Skeeter?"

"I was finished talking for a while," Skeeter says, looking down at his feet. I guess the sun is hurting his eyes. "How did you find me?"

"I didn't—the girls did," Ma says, pointing to all of us.

"Yeah—you two were always the smart ones. You could be detectives," Uncle Skeeter chuckles, scratching his head some more. Maybe he really *does* have lice!

"Well?" Ma says, like she's waiting for an explanation. "Daddy would turn over in his grave if he saw what you're doing to yourself."

"Yeah . . . well, that's why I guess I decided to join him, for a little peace and quiet. I'm tired of everybody telling me what I should be doing," Uncle Skeeter says defensively.

"So, that's your solution? Give up on your life and hurt all of us, just because we care about you?" Ma screams at the top of her lungs.

Uncle Skeeter breaks down, crying like a baby. "I thought maybe Daddy could give me some *answers*, Junie. I-I-I didn't know where to look anymore," he says, barely able to talk.

"What answers do you need, Skeeter?" Ma cries back.

"What to do with myself! I *hate* my life—my job—all of it. I don't want to pick up people's garbage anymore. My wife *hates* me. I can't afford to take care of my kids . . ."

"Stop feeling sorry for yourself, Skeeter!" Ma cries out.

"I'm so ashamed that y'all have to see me like this," Uncle Skeeter says, looking at us with embarrassed eyes. "These are your friends I heard about?"

Angie and I start crying. We're too choked up to answer.

"We're from New York," Galleria pipes up.

"I can see that," Uncle Skeeter says, peering at Galleria, Chanel, and Dorinda.

"Uncle Skeeter," I cry, running up to him and hugging him tight. "Don't leave us, ever again."

Uncle Skeeter heaves a deep, long sigh. "I won't, Nettie One. I promise. Not until the Good Lord takes me."

Chapter 11

Now that Uncle Skeeter is safe and sound, all we can think about is the Karma's Children benefit concert. We have taken two hours just to get ready, and it shows in the way we "prowl" to the backstage entrance of the Turtle Dome Arena.

The pathway is lit with beautiful Chinese paper lanterns that brighten the sky. Dragonflies swirl around the globes of light, giving off twinkle-dinkle sparkles every now and then.

As we push our way through the crowd to get to the "talent entrance," people are staring at us. "Oooo, look at their outfits!" we hear them saying. We smile at them, and Chanel even raises her hand into the "growl power" sign, which causes quite a few giggles.

"Are y'all performing?" one little girl asks us, as we try to move past the hordes of ticket holders.

"Yes, ma'am," Galleria says, leading the way behind Ma.

"Wait till Mr. Chips Carter gets a whiff of what's cooking!" I tease Ma. Since her cheetah-fied escapade worked, we talked her into wearing a leopard silk scarf around her neck tonight. She looks real pretty—and she even did her nails!

"Never mind, Nettie One—you just concentrate on getting your turns down right, and not hitting anyone with that fake money," Ma says, kinda bossy.

She can say whatever she wants—I *know* there is something cookin' between her and Mr. Chips Carter. And why not? He may not have money, but he has music. Besides, he's not bad-looking. He's not too old for Ma—and at least he has all his teeth!

"Do you think Uncle Skeeter is gonna show up?" Angie asks, concerned.

"He gave us his word."

"How old do you think those two are?"

Dorinda interrupts, staring at Houston's own kiddie rappers, Miggy and Mo'.

"They must be about Egyptian and India's age, ain't that right, Angie?" I ask.

"Yup."

"Who's Egyptian and India?" Chanel asks, obviously intrigued.

"They are our cousins," I exclaim. "Uncle Skeeter's daughters. You'll meet them, and Big Momma, and everybody else at Thanksgiving dinner."

"Ain't this like a dream come true?" Angie yells over the noise of the crowd.

"I'm not sure yet—wait till we get inside," I holler back. If we don't make our way through this mob and get into the arena soon, this night could turn into a Nightmare on Kemah Boardwalk!

"All these people paid fifty dollars for concert tickets?" Galleria asks in utter disbelief.

"Yes, ma'am," I tell her, as we approach the promised land—the backstage door. There we're stopped by a ten-foot-tall Mighty Man security guard. "Can I help you?" he asks.

"We—they—are perfoming for the benefit," Ma says, pointing to us. The Mighty Man looks us over, then lets us through. Even a dodo bird can see we are performing. Why else would be parading around in cheetah outfits?

Once we're back in the talent holding room, we plop down on the couch and wait for instructions. We wave hi to Miggy and Mo'. They are still wearing pigtails, and I can tell they've put makeup on to try and cover their freckles, but you can still see them!

"Hey!" yells Mr. Fred Fish, coming over with his arms outstretched to greet us.

"You ladies are the reason we are here," Mr. Chips Carter starts in. I look at him, puzzled. I wonder if Mrs. Fenilworth told him we got them into the show—but then I realize, he's just flirting again.

"'Cuz if you ladies weren't here, me and Fred woulda went and caught some deer!" Mr. Carter says, laughing loudly at his own joke. "'Cuz I got the lost-woman blues!"

Ma is just beaming from ear to ear. Mr. Chips Carter takes her hand and kisses it, like he's found gold! "That was some fine dinner last night, Ms. Junifred."

"Why thank you," Ma says. "We'll have to do it again sometime. . . ."

"Ahem. I wonder where Karma's Children's dressing room is?" Dorinda asks, diverting our attention from the grown-ups.

"You can bet it ain't in here, lovely lady," Mr. Fred Fish says, chuckling loudly, "'cuz stars always get dressing rooms as big as the Taj Mahal!"

"I wonder if they're here," Galleria muses.

"You'll know when they're here," Mr. Fish says, "because I have a notion there will be lots of commotion in the ocean!"

"Y'all are like rappers," Dorinda says, looking up at Fish 'N' Chips, amused.

"Lovely lady, before they even invented the word rap, we were rapping," Mr. Chips Carter says. "That's what the blues is all about—speaking your mind."

"And before you had rap, we had the snap *and* the tap," Mr. Fred Fish says, snapping his fingers and tapping his foot wildly. "*Yessiree.* We always had to find the rhythm *somewhere.*"

"I never thought about it that way," Galleria says, getting excited. She whips out her Kitty Kat notebook and starts scribbling in it madly.

"Yo, Galleria—you're like the mad scientist of lyrics," Dorinda chuckles.

"He's here!!" Angie says excitedly, pointing to the door.

Now it's my turn to scream. "Uncle Skeeter!"

"Ooh, look how nice you look!" Angie says, touching Uncle Skeeter's wild flowered shirt. He's also wearing a straw hat, and his shoes are spit-polished just the way he likes them.

"Fish 'N' Chips," I say excitedly, combining their names, "this is my Uncle Skeeter. He's into the blues too!"

Uncle Skeeter starts blushing, "Well . . ."

"Let's hear what you got!" Mr. Fish says, cutting him off. He whips out his banjo, and Mr. Carter takes out his tambourine.

"What's your name?"

"Skeeter Jasper," Uncle Skeeter says, pulling a harmonica out of his pants pocket.

"Omigod, I remember that thing!" Angie says.

I'd forgotten that Uncle Skeeter used to play the harmonica. Like I said before, he was always playing *something*. Mr. Fish and Mr. Chips pull up three chairs, and Uncle Skeeter sits on the one in the middle.

"Okay, now, Skeet—I'm gonna start in, then Chips, then you follow us," Mr. Fish starts strumming, nodding his head like he's in heaven. Mr. Chips joins right in, shaking his tambourine, tapping his foot. Uncle Skeeter starts blowing on his harmonica. Then Mr. Chips starts singing, "'I woke up this morning with a bad case of the lost-woman blues . . .'"

"'I said I woke up this morning . . .'" Mr. Fred Fish cuts in.

We start clapping our hands together, and Miggy and Mo' and the guys from the Moody Gardens band come over and join in. I look over at Ma, and I can see the tears welling up in her eyes.

All of sudden, we hear screaming. Dorinda runs to the doorway to see what's going on, then she comes running back. "They're here! *Karma's Children* are here—in the room right next to us!"

Uncle Skeeter and Fish 'N' Chips keep playing, but I have to run out and see if I can catch a glimpse of Karma's Children. I crane my neck, but all I see is a crowd clogging up the hallway. "Can *you* see them?" I ask the girl standing in front of me.

"No. They went inside the dressing room, and there's a security guard blocking the doorway."

"Too bad."

I go back and listen to Uncle Skeeter and Fish 'N' Chips do their thing.

"Look at how happy Uncle Skeeter looks," Angie says, squeezing my arm.

"I know. His whole face just lights up when he plays the harmonica.

"He's good, too."

"Well, of course," Ma butts in. "He's a Jasper!"

Miggy and Mo' come over and sit by us, eating tuna sandwiches and nodding along with their heads. Uncle Skeeter and the dynamic duo, Fish 'N' Chips, finally stop playing, and we all clap *real* loud, and scream, "Woop, woop," too.

"Well, Mr. Chips," Mr. Fred Fish says, "I think tonight Fish 'N' Chips is gonna be going on 'with special guest, Skeeter Jeeter.'"

"Jasper!" Ma shouts out, proud of her maiden name.

"Well, now, that's Jasper to you, but Jeeter to us," Mr. Fish says, nodding at Uncle Skeeter and Mr. Chips, and showing off those empty spaces where his front teeth used to be. Now I wonder what Fish 'N' Chips's *real* names are . . .

"Oh, word, I get it—a stage name! That's what he means," Dorinda says, smiling.

"Well, I like it," Ma says, nodding her head in approval.

We run over and hug Uncle Skeeter. "Well, I guess this has turned out to be a family affair," Ma says, smiling. Then, looking at Dorinda, Chanel, and Galleria, she adds, "Now don't forget that y'all are family too."

"Thank you, Mrs. Walker," Dorinda says, touched by Ma's generosity.

"Call me Junifred, sweetie," Ma tells her.

Galleria hands us each a batch of fake Benjamins. "Y'all, we should each hold on to our own Benjies."

"You said *'y'all!'*" I tease Galleria.

"I reckon I did, Miz 'Aquanetta does it betta!'" Galleria shoots back.

"I could sure use some of your eggnog right about now," Dorinda says.

"Wait till you taste *mine*," Ma says proudly. "We are going to have a good-time Thanksgiving, trust me!"

"Oh, no! We're first!" I moan, looking at the lineup for the warm-up acts. "I wish Ms. Dorothea were here. She'd set them straight! No offense to you, Ma."

"No offense taken," Ma quips back.

"We *hate* going on first," offers Miggy.

I just look at her. She's only nine or ten years old. How would she know? They've probably only been performing all of two days!

As if reading my mind, Angie asks Miggy, "How long have you two been performing?"

"Five years," Miggy says proudly. "We started when I was five and she was four."

"Oh," says Dorinda, shrinking into her chair.

"Listen, we're gonna be doing this gig at the Okie-Dokie Corral—" Mo' says.

"What's that?" Dorinda asks, squinching up her nose.

"It's the first urban rodeo," Miggy says.

"It's gonna be in Fort Bend County," Mo' volunteers.

"And they're looking for more talent—if you wanna try out for it," Miggy says, shrugging her shoulders.

"Let's do it!" Chanel says excitedly.

"Um, sorry," Ma tells them. "But these girls are headed back to New York City on Sunday."

"Ain't y'all from here?" Miggy asks.

"Originally," I say quickly, wanting to stop the conversation right there.

"Uncle Skeeter, Fish 'N' Chips—y'all should try out for it!" Angie exclaims, motioning for them to get the information.

"Well, why not? I always wanted to be a hot diggity cowboy!" Mr. Fish cackles loudly.

Now that show time is just around the bend, Galleria commands us, "Let's do the Cheetah Girls prayer!" We join hands and do our chant, which ends, "Whatever makes us clever, forever!" Then it's time to get into position backstage.

Uncle Skeeter winks at me and Angie. "Don't wear them out, Nettie One and Two. Leave some applause for us!"

We are ushered past production crew and guests standing in the hallway. I'm clutching the fake "Benjies" tightly in my hand. I feel jittery and jumpy. No matter how many times we've performed, whether it's in the church choir or at the Apollo Theatre, it's always scary.

Mrs. Fenilworth has taken the stage. "We have a long tradition of helping our own in Houston," she says, "and tonight we continue that tradition, by giving these singing groups the chance to show their talents. If there's anything we have here in Houston, it's Texas-sized talent."

The crowd roars, "Yeah, Houston! Yeah, Texas!"

"Our first guests are the Cheetah Girls, a singing group that hails from right here in Houston." (Now the rest of the Cheetah Girls know how Angie and I feel every time an M.C. says we're from New York.)

When we get onstage, I take a real good look at the crowd. I can't believe how many people there are! When the music track kicks in, Galleria opens her umbrella, Chanel and Dorinda huddle under it with her, and Angie and I stand next to them. After two beats, we begin singing "It's Raining Benjamins."

At the onset of the chorus, we throw the fake money into the audience and bounce around onstage:

"It's raining Benjamins,
for a change and some coins
It's raining Benjamins
I heard that
It's raining . . . again!"

The crowd goes wild! People are pushing each other trying to grab the fake "Benjies" that are floating through the air. After we finish the song and take our bow, we hightail it off the stage, just as we've been instructed. They're still applauding, long after we get backstage!

"I can't wait for the day when we can just stand there and go with the flow, 'cuz it's *our* show," Galleria says.

Miggy and Mo' are being ushered onstage. "Good luck!" I whisper to them. They wave back, smiling. They may be little, but they sure are pros!

"That's my girls!" Uncle Skeeter says when we get back to the holding area. He takes turns giving me and Angie hugs and "squiggles," like he used to when we were little. "I'm so proud of you two," he says, tears in his eyes.

"We're proud of you, too, Skeeter," Angie says.

"Are you gonna become part of Fish 'N' Chips?" I ask him.

"Well, why not?" Uncle Skeeter says, looking at Mr. Fish and Mr. Carter. "You know what? I finally figured out what I'm really tired of."

"What?" I ask, curious.

"I'm tired of not chasing *my* dreams," he says, wiping the sweat off his forehead. "I love the rhythm, you know—I guess it's in the Jasper blood—so I'm gonna have to 'go with that flow,' as your girl Galleria here would say."

We chuckle at how astute Uncle Skeeter is. He gets everybody's program *real* quick.

"I really dig your little group," he says, pointing to all five of us now. "When are y'all going back home?"

"Not until we get an autograph from Karma's Children—*and* a photo," Galleria huffs.

"Not until we go to the Galleria Mall and go window shopping!" Chanel smirks.

We turn to Dorinda to see what she's gonna say, but she just shrugs her shoulders and says, "Not until you kick me out."

Bless her little heart.

"And I *know* you're not going before you eat my Thanksgiving dinner!" Ma says, getting into the mix. "You know, I never knew what Aqua and Angie meant when they told me you girls had 'growl power'—but after watching you perform in front of five thousand people, I'll tell you this—ain't nobody gonna stop the Cheetah Girls!"

It's Raining Benjamins

For the first time in her-story
there's a weather forecast
that looks like the mighty cash.
So tie up your shoes and
put away your blues
'cuz we're going around the bend
at half past ten
to the only place in town
where everything is coming up green
You know what I mean:

It's raining Benjamins
for a change and some coins
It's raining Benjamins
I heard that, so let's make some noise
It's raining . . . again!

Now maybe you're wondering
what's all the thundering—
But we've got the root of all the loot
that got past Santa's chute
without collecting soot.

So put on your galoshes
and bring the noshes
to the only place in town
where money is falling on the ground
That's right, y'all:

It's raining Benjamins
for a change and some coins
It's raining Benjamins
I heard that
It's raining . . . again!

So here's the rest of the her-story
now that there's no longer a mystery.
It's the precipitation in the nation
that's causing all the sensation
in the only way that dollar bills
can give you thrills.
Yeah, that's what I mean:

It's raining Benjamins
for a change and some coins
It's raining Benjamins
I heard that, so make some noise
It's R-A-I-N-I-N-G . . . AGAIN!
(Say it, again! Okay . . .)

The Cheetah Girls Glossary

The blues: Heart-thumpin' music from back in the day. B. B. King and Muddy Waters are the kings of "snappin,' tappin'" blues music, but the legend of the blues will live forever.

Boostin': Jammin'.

Dee-vorced: Divorced. No longer married.

Get the rodeo on the road: Bounce. Make moves.

Hush the mush: Stop whining. Stop getting mushy.

Manners-impaired: Someone who is so clumsy that they keep stepping on your foot even though a blind crocodile could see it!

Mausoleum: A big, gloomy place where dead people are buried in cemeteries.

Pawnshop: A place where you can bring your valuable stuff when you're po' up from the floor up and they lend you some duckets and give you a pawnshop ticket for your belongings.

Sanitation department: Garbage collection.

Spookies: A bad case of creepy, crawly feelings. Also known as the "willies" and the "heebie-jeebies."

Squiggle: A hug with squealing and shaking involved.

PHOTO BY CHARLIE PIZZARELLO

ABOUT THE AUTHOR

Deborah Gregory earned her growl power as a diva-about-town contributing writer for ESSENCE, VIBE, and MORE magazines. She has showed her spots on several talk shows, including OPRAH, RICKI LAKE, and MAURY POVICH. She lives in New York City with her pooch, Cappuccino, who is featured as the Cheetah Girls' mascot, Toto.

PHOTO BY TREVOR BROWN

 JUMP AT THE SUN

the Cheetah Girls

Are the Cheetahs leaving the music scene?

As the **CHEETAH GIRLS** get ready to perform at an urban rodeo with their arch rivals, Cash Money Girls, the **GIRLS** are accused of plagiarizing their lyrics.

Can the **CHEETAHS** prove themselves innocent in time for the big showdown?

stay tuned in

Cheetah Girls #9: Showdown at the Okie-Dokie

arriving
october 2000

Hey, Girlfriend!

Would you like to be a member of our club?

Join Today!